YOU SAVE THE WORLD ADVENTURE #1

DAVID BLAZE

COVER DESIGN BY YUSUP MEDIYAN
ILLUSTRATIONS BY POTTERNSM

Published by David Blaze

www.davidblazebooks.com

ISBN Paperback: 978-1-7334775-3-6

For Zander Blaze and
Every Young Superhero,

The greatest superpowers are honesty and
integrity, but these will have to do for
now...

Other Books
for Junior Readers
by David Blaze

Epic Kids

My Fox Ate My Homework

My Fox Ate My Cake

My Fox Ate My Alarm Clock

My Cat Ate My Homework

My Fox Begins

My Fox Ate My Report Card

My Fox, My Friend Forever

Janie Gets A Genie For Christmas

Introduction

(Do Not Skip This)

This is a gamebook that allows you to control the story. You will have choices to make after every scene. Those choices will determine how the story goes for you. Keep reading pages forward (like a regular book) until you see a selection of choices. They will direct you to the next page number you should go to. Notice that the page numbers are in the upper corners of each page.

There is a main menu on page 6. You can always return to it if you want to start over or try another superpower. Don't think you can cheat by skipping ahead to page 6. The story won't make any sense if you do that.

There are 46 endings and they don't all end with saving the day. That's part of playing this game. If at first you don't succeed, try again and again. That's how you win video games, right? Use that same mindset here. You get better each time you play because you learn what to do and what not to do.

It's time to save the day and become a superhero. Are you ready to find out what's inside? Maybe you'll become faster or stronger or you'll fly or teleport or walk through walls or freeze time or even shapeshift into a marvelous creature.

And to help you on your journey, you're getting the ability to time travel backwards right now. Use it wisely.

Ready? Let's go!

YOU'RE STANDING ALONE in a room you've never been in before. There are no doors and there are no windows. The walls around you are white with wooden shelves full of shiny new lab equipment.

You've got to focus and find a way out of here because your friends outside are in great danger and you're the only one who can save them.

You open your right hand and stare at the four vials full of glowing liquid you're holding. These are the keys to saving your friends.

5 MINUTES AGO …

THIS IS THE WEEKEND you're staying at Kim and
Kevin's house, your new friends from across the street. The
twin siblings turned twelve years old today. It's supposed to be
a fun birthday weekend with them that includes movies,
games, popcorn, and pizza, but this is turning into something
far from that.

Their father, Dr. Francis, is a medical research scientist. He
wears a black tie and rolls up his sleeves. He came home from
an international conference today, snatched Kim's pet mouse
cage from the living room, then rushed into his office and
closed the door behind him without a word.

"What's he doing with the mouse?" you asked the twins.

"Daddy is working on a secret project," Kim said, keeping
her eyes on the car racing video game the three of you were
playing. She has a long ponytail that goes all the way down her
back. "He'll get me another mouse. He always does." You
couldn't help but wonder what kind of secret project involved
a mouse—especially that mouse. It's old, slow, and can't walk
more than two steps before losing its breath.

Kevin paused the game and set his video controller on the
floor. He always wears his cap backwards. "We know better
than to disturb him when he gets this way."

"Was that your father?" Mrs. Francis asked as she stuck her
head out of the kitchen. She has short brown hair and wears
big round glasses. The twins nodded. "Let him know dinner

will be ready in a minute." She disappeared back into the kitchen, leaving the twins and you to determine who would be the messenger.

"We're friends, right?" Kim asked you, restarting the game without telling anyone. She swayed her body toward you as her race car drifted past Kevin's on the eighty-inch TV. "Will you do it? Please?"

"Yeah," you said. Your car crashed because you weren't ready.

"Friends for life," Kevin added as he grabbed his controller and tried to catch up with his sister's car. "Cheater!" he shouted at her.

You took a deep breath and headed down the hall to Dr. Francis's office. You had never talked to him before because he had been away on scientific trips and conferences around the world. You knocked on his door three times and waited. He didn't answer so you knocked again and called out his name. He still didn't answer.

After a moment of hesitation you cracked the door open. Dr. Francis was on the other side of the room with his back to you, the mouse cage on a table in front of him. He appeared to be feeding the mouse from a glass vial.

The door squeaked as you pushed it forward slowly.

Dr. Francis turned to you, the blood in his face drained. That's when things got crazy. The old, slow mouse jumped into the mouse wheel and ran faster than you had ever seen any animal run.

"You're not supposed to be here," Dr. Francis blurted. The mouse wheel squealed behind him as it spun in circles faster and faster. "No one's supposed to be here." He grabbed a blue towel and threw it over the cage, covering it completely.

You pointed to the open door behind you and explained, "Mrs. Francis said dinner is almost ready."

He shook his head and marched around you to the door, muttering, "I thought it was locked ... why isn't it locked?" He closed the door, locked it, and faced you. "How much did you see?"

Tires skidded in the driveway outside before you could answer. Dr. Francis rushed to a window facing the front yard and pulled the curtains back. You watched with him as a young woman with long red hair stepped out of a yellow sports car.

"She figured it out," Dr. Francis whispered. His hands were shaking. "She came for the vials."

He closed the curtains and ran to a computer desk in the corner of the room. He punched in five numbers on the keyboard then looked at you and sighed as the wall behind the mouse cage split open and revealed a hidden room with white walls and wooden shelves.

"Follow the passage into my secret lab," he said. "You're our only hope." He handed you the same vial he had fed the mouse with. It was empty but had glowing yellow residue from whatever liquid had been in it. "There are four more like this in there. You must destroy them all." Sweat poured from his forehead. "Ava can never find these, or all is lost."

"Wait," you insisted as he guided you to the hidden room. More tires skidded in the driveway outside. "I don't understand."

"I have to protect my family," he said as he pushed you into the lab. He went back to his computer and punched in five more numbers as someone pounded a fist on the office door.

FIND THE VIALS! DESTROY THEM ALL!

The wall closed in as quickly as it had opened, sealing you inside.

NOW

VOICES OUTSIDE THIS SECRET LAB are impossible to understand through the wall. You don't know what's happened to Dr. Francis or even if the twins and Mrs. Francis are safe.

The other glowing vials are hovering over an oval display, suspended in air. You cautiously grab them with both hands and hold them up to the light above you. Each one has a label around it. The vial the mouse drank from says ZIP. That makes sense, but the others are a mystery. Three are labelled MASK, EMIT, and TOWER. The last one has no label on it.

You lose your balance while looking up and stumble into one of the lab shelves. Scales and hotplates crash onto the floor with tremendous clatter, bangs, and thuds.

"Over there!" a woman's voice shouts, likely Ava. "Open it!"

The wall begins to split down the middle. You have seconds before Ava is inside and you have no idea what she will do with the vials or even what she will do with you. Maybe, just maybe the liquid in the vials will protect you by making you faster like the mouse or stronger or smarter.

What do you do? You have four vials to select from or you can destroy them like Dr. Francis told you to. Think fast! This is the most important decision of your life.

>>Turn the page to make your selection<<

MAKE YOUR SELECTION NOW!

If you drink from the green vial labelled
MASK, turn to page 7

If you drink from the orange vial labelled
EMIT, turn to page 10

If you drink from the blue vial labelled
TOWER, turn to page 15

If you drink from the purple vial with
NO LABEL, turn to page 18

If you **Destroy All of The Vials,**
turn to page 21

YOU UNCAP THE VIAL labelled MASK, throw your head back, and swallow the green glowing liquid in one big gulp. You slam the other vials on the floor and crush them beneath your shoes. The liquid turns into a cloud of colorful smoke and evaporates.

Your whole body tingles the way your hand does when you accidentally sleep on it and it tries to wake back up.

You stare straight ahead, frozen in place, as Ava enters the lab with a large man in a military uniform. They march straight toward you.

Ava stops in front of the broken vials and holds the man back. She slips a protective mask over her mouth and nose and instructs him to do the same.

He affixes a mask to his monstrous face and approaches the shelves with hotplates and scales. After studying each item with interest, he throws them off the shelves one by one. He grunts each time, disappointed he doesn't find what he's looking for.

"That's enough, Captain," Ava says to him. "Whoever was here destroyed the vials. Let's go. I have experiments to run on the children."

You're astonished as they walk away from you like you're not even here. It's almost like you're invisible. Wait a minute ... look at your hands ... there's nothing there ... you are invisible!

"I set the bomb for five minutes," the captain says in his booming voice from the doctor's office. "All evidence must be destroyed."

You have to see for yourself what's going on. Don't just stand there. Move!

You run back into the office just as the front door closes when Ava and the captain leave the house. You're horrified to find a bomb that looks like sticks of dynamite tied together on the table where the mouse cage was. Red numbers are counting down on it. Mrs. Francis is sitting on the floor with her hands and legs tied.

"Mrs. Francis," you call out to her. "Are you okay?"

She looks around the room in confusion. "Who said that? Where are you?"

"It's me," you say. "Kim and Kevin's friend. I drank one of Dr. Francis's vials. I don't think anyone can see me now."

Even though she can't see you, you shake your head no because there's no way you're leaving her here with the bomb. You go to her and try to untie her hands, but you can't. The knots are different from any you've ever seen before.

"Where are Kim and Kevin?" you ask her.

"They're safe," she assures you. "They're in a safe room. My husband likes to call it a panic room."

You stand back in frustration because you can't untie the knots and time is running out. There are twenty-six seconds left on the bomb's timer.

"You're a good kid," Mrs. Francis says, "but I'm begging you to leave me behind. I can make it out of here. Really, I can." You doubt that's true because she can't even move. "If that woman leaves with my husband's secrets, then the whole world is in danger. Go!"

To stay with Mrs. Francis,
Turn to page 24.

To stop Ava and the captain,
Turn to page 38.

YOU UNCAP THE VIAL labelled EMIT, throw your head back, and swallow the orange glowing liquid in one big gulp. You slam the other vials on the floor and crush them beneath your shoes. The liquid turns into a cloud of colorful smoke and disappears.

Your head turns involuntarily from side to side at lightning speed. It feels like you're moving all over the lab though you're standing in place. You close your eyes and wish you were anywhere but here as Ava steps into the lab with a large man in a military uniform.

"This isn't good," Ava says, but she sounds far away, like she's in another room.

You slowly reopen one eye just a fraction, hoping she can't see you looking at her. But you don't see her. You see a table with a blue towel on it—the same table and the same blue towel you saw in Dr. Francis's office. The mouse cage is gone and solid wooden tubes with red digital numbers are on the table.

Wait. This is his office. That's his desk over there. How did you get in here? And where is Dr. Francis?

"Put your mask on, Captain," Ava says from another room.

You arch your neck around the table and see through the open wall leading to the lab. Ava and the captain have their backs to you.

The captain slips a mask over his huge face and begins to toss everything off the shelves. You're not sure if he's looking for more vials or if he's just angry.

"That's enough, Captain," Ava says to him. "The vials are already destroyed. Let's go. I have experiments to run on the children."

What is she going to do to you and your friends? Worry about that later. Ava and the captain are heading back in this direction, straight for you.

You can't leave the house yet because you've got to find out what happened to your friends and their parents. You take a deep breath, close your eyes, and focus your mind on the secret lab. Now reopen your eyes. You're back in the lab and watch Ava and the captain walk out.

"I set the bomb for five minutes," the captain says in his booming voice. "All evidence must be destroyed."

You can't breathe. The objects with red digital numbers you saw on the table are a bomb and it's going to explode in five minutes. You've got to find your friends and get out of here as quickly as possible.

You jump into action when you hear the front door open and then close after Ava and the captain leave. You rush out of the lab and stop at the table to see the red numbers counting down. They currently show 04:36. "Four minutes and thirty-six seconds," you whisper. Your heart is racing. "That's enough time. It has to be."

You run to the window by the front door and watch Ava's yellow sports car and a camouflaged van peel out of the driveway. You run through the house, searching for your friends room by room, and calling out their names. "Kim!

Kevin! Dr. Francis! Mrs. Francis!"

They're not anywhere in the house. There's nowhere else to look. This is good. Maybe they got out and they're safe.

You take a moment to bend over and catch your breath. It occurs to you that Dr. Francis's computer can do amazing things. It opened up the secret lab and sealed you inside. Maybe your friends are in another secret room.

You run back into the office and try to log in to the computer but it's locked with a password. The red numbers on the bomb show 03:07. "If I was a genius, what would my password be?" You put in the wrong password twice and have one try left.

You're ready to give up because there's no way you can guess his password. "Maybe...." Today is Kim and Kevin's birthday. Maybe the password isn't a word. Maybe it's numbers. And maybe those numbers are today's date—their birthday.

You put in today's date using two numbers for the month, two numbers for the day of the month, and four numbers for the year. It works!

There are three folders named LAB, WORK, and PANIC on the monitor. The red numbers on the bomb show 02:15. "Panic is what I'm doing right now," you mumble. You click on that folder and gasp.

A live video plays of your friends and Mrs. Francis in a room you've never seen before. You focus on the room's details. There's a stockpile of canned food in the back. There are four cots to lie on. There are pictures of birds on the walls. There aren't any widows. You close your eyes and imagine being there. Now open your eyes again.

Kim, Kevin, and Mrs. Francis are in front of you. You reach out and hug them all, relieved to see that they're okay.

"How did you…" Mrs. Francis starts to say.

"Where's our dad?" Kim interrupts.

You shrug and say, "I don't know. There's a bomb in your house and he's not there."

"They took him away," Mrs. Francis says, sitting on a cot as if she's exhausted. "But we're still in the house. This is a safe room. My husband likes to call it a panic room. We came here when he warned us."

You know there's not much time left on the bomb. "We need to leave—now."

"We're not going anywhere," Mrs. Francis says, reaching for Kim and Kevin. "We can't. This room locks automatically for two hours with no way in or out. It's for our protection." She hugs the twins close. "Don't worry. It was made to withstand all natural disasters and home invasions. We'll be safe here."

Her words are convincing but you sense doubt in her eyes, like she's not sure she believes her own words. "I know about my husband's work," she admits to you. "And I see that you can teleport. He's not supposed to talk about what he does, but … yeah."

"You knew about this?" Kevin asks, sounding like he feels

betrayed.

Mrs. Francis pats his head and focuses on you. "We'll be fine here. Your ability to teleport won't last forever. You need to go right now."

You don't want to leave them. Kim is huddled close to her mom. Kevin nods at you like he's saying goodbye for the last time.

You don't know how much time is left—maybe seconds. What if you can grab the bomb and teleport with it to another location, a place where no one can get hurt? It's a risk. If you go back into the office, you may find that the bomb is out of time and explodes on you.

To teleport to safety in your own home,
turn to page 35.

To teleport to the bomb,
turn to page 41.

YOU UNCAP THE VIAL labelled TOWER, throw your head back, and swallow the blue glowing liquid in one big gulp. You slam the other vials on the floor and crush them beneath your shoes. The liquid turns into a cloud of colorful smoke and disappears.

Your stomach rumbles. Your head spins.

Ava steps into the lab and looks around just as you lose your balance again. Your body feels weightless and lifts up into the air, higher and higher. Your back bumps against the ceiling and you stay there, flat, motionless as a large man in a military uniform appears behind Ava.

Ava stops directly beneath you at the crushed vials and holds a hand back for the man to stay behind her. "Put your mask on, Captain," she advises as she puts one over her own mouth and nose.

He slips a mask over his huge face and begins to throw everything off the shelves. You can tell he's searching for something specific, maybe more vials. He doesn't find anything and glances over the walls and looks up toward the ceiling.

"That's enough," Ava says to him. "Whoever was here destroyed the vials. Let's go. I have experiments to run on the children."

Every muscle in your body feels numb. What is she going to do to Kim and Kevin? You've got to find a way down to help them.

Ava and the captain walk out of the room and back into

Dr. Francis's office. "I set the bomb for five minutes," the captain says in a booming voice. "All evidence must be destroyed."

"What about the doctor?" Ava asks.

"All evidence must be destroyed," the captain repeats.

You swing your arms and legs, fighting to get down as they leave the house. You have less than five minutes to get out of here before the bomb explodes. You've got to save yourself and Dr. Francis and find out where the rest of the family is.

Nothing is working. You can't get down. You have no idea how much time has passed. Maybe two minutes? Maybe three?

You close your eyes, take a deep breath, and repeat, "Down, down, down." You reopen your eyes and see the floor is coming at you fast. You shield your face with your arms before you crash onto the floor.

Your body hovers over the floor at the last second, less than an inch above it. You clumsily bend your legs and stand up straight. You pause and try to figure out how you did it but then you rush out of the room to help Dr. Francis and his family.

He's sitting on the office floor with his legs tied in front of him and his hands tied behind him. The computer he used to open the wall with is gone. The mouse cage is also gone and what looks like dynamite sticks with red digital numbers have replaced it on the blue towel.

You rip duct tape off Dr. Francis's mouth and begin to untie his legs. You haven't seen the kind of knots the rope is

tied in before—it's twisted in a way you can't undo.

Red numbers on the bomb's timer show there are fifty-nine seconds left before it explodes.

The bomb continues counting down quickly. You can fly, right? Maybe you don't know how to do it but you can do it. If you can't get Dr. Francis untied, maybe there's a way you can get the bomb out of here and fly it off to a safe location.

"Go!" Dr. Francis shouts as the timer reaches thirty seconds.

To stay and help Dr. Francis, turn to page 28.

To fly off with the bomb, turn to page 42.

YOU UNCAP THE VIAL WITH NO LABEL, throw your head back, and swallow the purple glowing liquid in one big gulp. You slam the other vials on the floor and crush them beneath your shoes. The liquid turns into a cloud of colorful smoke and disappears.

Your clothes are tighter around your arms and legs and looser around your stomach. You're taller because you're standing up straighter than ever before.

Ava steps into the lab and stares at you with cold eyes as a large man in a military uniform joins her. "What have you done?" she says as she walks up to you and kicks the shattered vials. She puts a protective mask over her mouth and nose and advises the man to do the same.

He slips a mask over his huge face and begins to toss everything off the shelves like they don't weigh anything. You duck when a hotplate flies at your head. He seems angry that he can't find whatever he's looking for.

"That's enough, Captain," Ava says to him. "The vials are already destroyed. Let's go. I have experiments to run on the children." She looks at you and smirks. "You think you're smart, don't you? My first experiment is going to be on you."

You feel numb. What is she going to do to you? You've got to find a way to get away from her and help your friends. She grabs your arm and leads you out of the lab and back into Dr. Francis's office.

You're shocked to find the doctor sitting on the floor with his hands and legs tied. His mouth is covered in duct tape. You also notice the mouse cage is gone and thick sticks with red digital numbers have replaced it on the table.

"The kid's coming with us," Ava says, squeezing your arm. It seems like your arm should hurt, but you don't feel anything. It's like she's not even touching it. "What do we do with the doctor?"

"All evidence must be destroyed," the captain repeats. "The clock is ticking. Time to go."

Ava pulls on your arm to lead you out of the house, but you resist and slip away from her. You feel stronger than ever. Maybe it's adrenaline because you sense Dr. Francis's life is in danger and you've got to save him.

The captain marches toward you like a beast and you put your hands out to protect yourself. Your hands hit his chest, and his body flies back and onto the floor in a heap.

"You drank one," Ava gasps. "It works." She approaches you carefully with her hands up to show she's not a threat. "You and I can change the world."

The bomb counts down to four minutes.

"Where are my friends?" you ask her. "Where is Mrs. Francis?" If they're in the house, you've got to get them out.

"Don't worry about them," she says. "They'll be fine, just fine." She reaches out a hand for you to grab. "Come with me and no one will get hurt."

To leave with Ava,
turn to page 32.

To stay and help Dr. Francis,
turn to page 44.

YOU SMASH THE GLASS VIALS on the floor and watch as the glowing liquid evaporates in a foggy haze of mixed colors.

The wall in front of you opens and Ava steps into the lab with a large man in a military uniform. "Why?" Ava asks as she stands in front of you and the broken vials. "Why would you do this?" She puts a protective mask over her mouth and tells the man to do the same. You instinctively put your hand over your mouth and nose.

The military man wraps a mask around his ginormous head and says, "You shouldn't have done that." He marches to the shelves full of lab equipment and tosses all of it onto the floor, one at a time. He's searching for something specific.

"That's enough, Captain," Ava says after a minute. "There aren't any more vials in here. Let's go. I have experiments to run on the children." She looks over your arms and legs and studies your eyes. "My first experiment is going to be on you." She grabs your arm and leads you back into the office you were in minutes ago with Dr. Francis.

The mouse cage is gone from the table and bundled dynamite sticks with blue, red, and white wires have taken its place. Dr. Francis is sitting on the floor with his hands tied behind him and his legs tied in front of him.

"I'm sorry," Dr. Francis mutters as the captain pushes you past him. "This wasn't supposed to happen."

You dig in your heels and face him. You don't know what's going on, but there's one thing you can't get off your mind.

"Where are Kim and Kevin? And Mrs. Francis? Are they okay?"

He sighs and says, "When you see them, do whatever you can to save them." Ava yanks on your arm and pulls you forward. You sense she doesn't want you to hear what Dr. Francis has to say. "Don't come back for me. Whatever you do, don't come back."

The captain pulls out a roll of duct tape, rips off a strip, and presses it over Dr. Francis's mouth. "I'm tired of listening to him," he says. He pulls a remote controller out of his pocket and presses a button. "I set the bomb for five minutes."

You suddenly realize what the wooden objects with wires are as Ava pushes you forward and out of the room in a hurry. "Wait!" you shout at her. "What about Dr. Francis?" She doesn't answer and forces you out of the house.

Now you're standing in front of the yellow sports car you saw earlier from the office window. There's a green, brown, and gray camouflaged military van parked behind it. Ava is still outside with you, holding your arm so you can't get away. You see that Kim, Kevin, and Mrs. Francis are in the back seat of the car, locked in. There's a glass barricade keeping them from the front.

"Get in the car," Ava says, pointing to it. "Front seat. Now's not the time for questions."

"They should be in the van," the captain says, shaking his head. "A lot more room."

"They're my responsibility, Captain," she responds angrily.

"Why are you doing this?" you ask her. "Why can't you just let us go?"

She pulls you away as the captain leans against his van and laughs. "Look, kid, you've been exposed to whatever was in those vials. We have a doctor who can make sure you're not infected." She seems sincere but you don't understand why she left Dr. Francis behind.

"Time to go!" the captain shouts as he jumps into the van.

Ava turns to the open van door. "Just go! The kid's coming with me!" You realize she's distracted and her hand isn't tight on your arm. This may be your only chance to run away. You still have time to save Dr. Francis before the bomb explodes, even though he told you not to. But if you do, you may never have a chance to save Kim, Kevin, and Mrs. Francis.

You have less than a second to decide before Ava turns back to you and tightens her grip. What do you do?

To rush back into the house to save Dr. Francis, turn to page 37.

To get into the car for a chance to save your friends, turn to page 46.

YOU REFUSE TO LEAVE Mrs. Francis here alone and focus on untying the knots around her legs. There's a blue wire and a red wire hanging from the bomb. You wonder if you can cut one of them and save the day. "Maybe I can diffuse the bomb."

"Don't even think about it," she admonishes. "Forget whatever you've seen on TV. Any wire you cut will make the bomb explode."

You wipe sweat from your forehead as seventeen seconds appear on the timer.

"Go," Mrs. Francis cries. "Please go."

You look around the room for anything that can loosen or cut the rope from her wrists and legs. You pause when you see the open wall leading to the secret lab. It's meant to stay hidden and secure so no one and nothing can go in or out without a code. Maybe the lab is reinforced to protect the home from … explosions.

"What's the code?" you ask Mrs. Francis, guessing she knows.

"What?" she asks, sounding confused.

"To close the wall," you say impatiently.

"01010," she says. "It's the binary code for the number 10—my husband's favorite number."

You rush to the table and pick the bomb up with both hands. It weighs as much as a backpack full of books. Don't look at the red numbers because they will only freak you out. Now move as fast as you can back into the lab and lay the bomb down in the middle of it. Good! Now run for your life!

You're back in the office now. You stop at the desk and swipe the computer mouse back and forth so the monitor wakes up. Three folders appear on the screen, but you don't have time to check them out. You quickly punch the numbers 01010 on the keyboard and turn to face the wall.

It's closing slowly. You don't think you've ever seen anything move so slowly in your life. This is worse than waiting for a pot of water to boil.

You cover Mrs. Francis's body with your own when the bomb explodes with a BOOM. The wall closes completely just as shrapnel hurls into it like a kazillion bullets. The walls around you shake like a rattlesnake and the vibrations from the floor rattle your bones.

"Are we alive?" you ask Mrs. Francis when the room stops moving.

"Yes," she says, "thanks to you." The rope around her wrists and legs is looser after all of that. You're finally able to untie her before she jumps up and goes to the computer.

You follow her as she clicks on one of the folders named PANIC. A live video plays and shows Kim and Kevin in a room with canned food and cots.

"Thank goodness," Mrs. Francis says, sighing in relief. "They're okay. They made it."

"We should get them out," you tell her. "It's not safe here."

"We can't," she explains. "Not yet. The room is locked for their protection for two hours." Sirens roar from down the street.

"What do I do about this?" you ask, placing a hand on her shoulder, knowing she can feel it but can't see it.

"It won't last forever," she assures you as she steps away from the computer and walks out the front door.

"Where are you going?" you ask, bewildered.

I WON'T LET THEM HURT MY HUSBAND. I KNOW WHERE THEY'RE TAKING HIM.

"Shouldn't we wait for the police?" you point out.

"There's not enough time," she argues.

To leave with Mrs. Francis, turn to page 50.

To stay and talk to the police, turn to page 73.

YOU CLOSE YOUR EYES and again focus on the stockpile of canned food, four cots, and pictures of birds. Now open your eyes. Everything looks the same but Kim, Kevin, and Mrs. Francis are not here. The room door must have unlocked during the blast or the firefighters got them out.

This is great news!

You close your eyes and prepare to teleport back outside. You picture the yard and the firetruck and police. You can't wait to see your friends. Now open your eyes again.

Wait. Something's wrong. You're still in the panic room.

You freak out for a moment. Try to breathe. Why didn't it work? Maybe it was just a glitch—try again. Close your eyes and think of your bedroom. Okay, reopen them.

You're staring at pictures of birds and a stockpile of food. Stay calm. Think. Maybe you can't teleport anymore but you can still walk out of this room.

The door won't open. The knob won't even budge a centimeter. You bang with all your might on the door and shout from the top of your lungs so anyone outside can hear you. Your voice and the bangs echo throughout the room. It is soundproof. No one can hear you, and you can't hear them.

You sit on one of the cots and look over the stockpile of food and water. It's enough to last for a few months. That's a good thing because you may be here for a very long time—maybe the rest of your life.

>>time travel back to page 36<<
THE END

YOU IGNORE DR. FRANCIS because you're not going to leave him here alone with the ticking bomb. The rope around his legs is getting tighter the more you pull on it. You're focused on his legs so he can get to his feet and run.

You think about all the times you've tied and untied your shoelaces and how it wasn't easy at first. You focus on the loops around this rope and push them through the knot.

It's working!

You loosen the rope around Dr. Francis's legs and throw it off him. You help him to his feet and rush with him to the front door as the bomb beeps with five seconds left.

Your heart is racing as you approach the front door. You pull it open and push Dr. Francis out in front of you.

The bomb screeches.

You're barely through the door when the whole house shakes like it's about to jump off the ground and the windows blow out in a million shattered pieces. The force of the explosion throws you to the ground and on top of the doctor.

The yellow sports car and a green, brown, and gray camouflaged military van race out of the yard and onto the highway. The doctor watches while he stumbles to his feet. "No!" he shouts as he heads for his car. He falls to his knees with his head in his hands when he sees that all of the tires are slashed.

"We need to call the police," you tell him.

He looks up at you and shakes his head. You can already hear sirens from far away. "Tell me you destroyed the vials."

"I did," you assure him. "Well, most of them."

He stands up and puts his hands on your shoulders. "What do you mean? Does Ava have one of them?"

"Not exactly," you say. "I'm sorry. I saw what the mouse could do. I drank one of them."

He's staring at you with big eyes, like he can't believe you would do something so foolish. "Why would you … never mind. It's already done." He sighs and says, "Which one did you drink?"

"The blue one," you tell him. "Tower."

He cracks his neck and runs a hand through his hair. "Do

you know what I do for a living?"

"You're a medical research scientist," you say, remembering what Kim and Kevin told you.

"Right, I run studies and trials to prevent and treat diseases," he confirms.

"Oh, cool," you say, not sure if it's really cool.

"I discovered something," he says. "Something impossible." He looks around the yard like he wants to make sure no one else is listening. "I found a way to alter the DNA of mice, giving them the ability to fight off almost any disease. But it has peculiar side effects."

"Side effects like flying?" you ask.

He winks at you. "I've modified it dozens of times, but different side effects keep appearing." The sirens are getting closer. "The vial you drank from was not meant for humans. It will take me years to work out the kinks and know how to eliminate the side effects."

"Why would you want to?" you wonder out loud.

He gives you a weak smile. "I tried to hide this project from my assistant. She works with me but is more dedicated to advancing the strength of the military than helping the average person in need."

"Ava," you whisper.

He nods. "If militaries had this power ... well, no one should have this power." He grabs your shoulders again. "Listen to me. I don't know how long you'll be able to fly. Maybe an hour. Maybe the rest of your life. That vial was meant for a mouse." He looks over you from head to toe. "With someone your size and your height, my best guess is that it will work for half an hour."

"I have time to catch up with them," you realize. "I can lead the police there."

"That's not a good idea," he warns. "You don't know how to fly. You need time to practice."

"There's not enough time for that. I can save Kim, Kevin, and Mrs. Francis," you say, taking a step back.

He puts his hands out and says, "They may be okay. We have a panic room behind the kitchen pantry reinforced with steel and Kevlar in case there's ever a tornado or home invasion. I sent my wife and kids a signal from my computer to seal themselves inside. It will not reopen for two hours."

"But we don't know for sure," you tell him. Ava said there were experiments to run on the children. "I have to go in case they've been taken."

"It could be dangerous. Please don't do it," Dr. Francis says.

To fly away and find the vehicles, turn to page 52.

To wait for police and fire rescue, turn to page 216.

"**DISABLE THE BOMB,** Captain," Ava says when you reluctantly agree to leave with her. You know you're never supposed to go with strangers but this is a matter of life and death. "Keep the doctor tied up until I call you from the research lab."

"What?" you say. "That's not what we agreed to."

She motions toward the front door. "Don't worry. Just do what I ask you to and he won't be harmed." She sighs and shakes her head. "But if you get any funny ideas like running away and asking someone for help, then…." She clasps her hands in front of her in a tight circle then pulls them apart quickly and says, "Boom."

Dr. Francis nods at you as you walk out of the room with Ava behind you. You hate leaving him here, but you're waiting for the right moment to use your newfound strength. You have no idea how to disable a bomb and this is the only way you can keep him safe.

Now that you're outside, you see a camouflaged military van parked behind Ava's sports car. As you walk past it, you glance inside and verify your friends and Mrs. Francis aren't in there.

"Looking for something?" Ava asks, nudging you forward. You shake your head and stop at the front passenger's door of her car. She's standing across from you at the driver's door and mimics a bomb exploding with her hands again.

You don't say anything once you're both inside the car and driving away. You're questioning if you made the right choice and if you could have done things differently.

Ava breaks the silence and says,

You shake your head. "Friends don't blow each other up," you mumble.

"Friends don't abandon each other either," she replies angrily. "Look, Dr. Francis and I were doing medical research for the military. He discovered something that can change the world and he kept it from the military. He kept it from me."

You imagine she's talking about the vials and what was inside of them. She must know that they can make you stronger. One can make you faster. You wonder what the others do and you wonder how the military would use them.

"He had no right to keep his findings from us," Ava says, turning to you with a scowl. "You had no right to destroy the vials." She takes a deep breath and smiles. "That's okay though. We've got his personal computer with all of his research now. And you're just the right age to do the testing on."

"I have to pee," you blurt when you see a gas station ahead. "Really bad." You realize that this problem with Ava, the captain, Dr. Francis and his family is much bigger than you can deal with on your own. There's got to be a way to get help.

Ava pulls the car into the gas station parking lot. You start to open your door when you see a woman in a security uniform inside the store. Ava grabs your arm before you get out.

"Come right back," she says. "Don't be a hero." She holds her cell phone up to her ear. "All I have to do is call the captain and the bomb keeps ticking down."

To go inside the store for help,
turn to page 82.

To stay in the car,
turn to page 85.

YOU TELL MRS. FRANCIS you'll call the police and fire department when you get home, but she says there's no need for that. Her husband would have already contacted them through his computer. You hug them and assure them you'll be waiting outside when the room door opens.

You close your eyes and imagine your house across the street and your bedroom. Now open your eyes again. There's your bed and the dirty clothes on your floor. You run to your window and look out to the Francises' house.

Sirens roar from down the street.

Help is coming…

There's a deafening *BOOM* and the ground shakes. All the windows in the Francises' house shatter and burst into a million fragments, followed by raging black smoke.

You dash out of your room and out of the house without even thinking. You have to know if your friends are okay. A fire truck reaches the yard before you and the firefighters keep you back.

Police arrive and tell everyone to stay out of the yard for their own safety while the firefighters are working. You look around and see the whole neighborhood is outside.

A short female officer appears. You want to tell her exactly what happened with Ava and the captain but aren't sure it's a good idea. It's all a little crazy and unbelievable. Plus, you're itching to teleport back into the panic room to check on the family, but you're scared of what you'll find.

To teleport back into the panic room,
turn to page 27.

To talk to the police,
turn to page 75.

YOU PULL AWAY FROM AVA and feel the whoosh of her hand as she tries to grab you. Not a chance! You make a mad dash for the house.

"Let's go!" the captain shouts from the van. "We're out of time!"

You make it through the front door, slam it shut, and lock it. You gasp for air because you ran like rattlesnakes were chasing you. You stare out the door's peephole and watch as the sports car and military van peel out of the driveway.

You turn and face the hallway that leads to Dr. Francis's office, knowing you have to move fast. The bomb was set for five minutes and you have no idea how much time has passed.

You race down the hall and into the office. Dr. Francis isn't sitting on the floor anymore. You frantically search the room for him. He's nowhere. You remember he said not to come back for him. Maybe he had another way out. Maybe he had another secret passage.

The timer on the bomb shows four seconds are left. You watch the red numbers flash quickly and wonder if things would have been different if you had gone with Kim, Kevin, and Mrs. Francis.

3 ....

2 ...

1 ...

>>time travel back to page 23<<
THE END

YOU RESPECT MRS. FRANCIS'S WISH and rush out of the house to find Ava and the captain talking. Her yellow sports car is out here and a large, camouflaged military van is parked behind it. The driver's door is open on the van so you look inside. There are two rows of seats in the back and Dr. Francis is sitting in the middle of the first one.

You climb over the driver's seat and sit next to him. His wrists and legs are tied just like Mrs. Francis's. There's duct tape over his mouth.

"Dr. Francis," you whisper. "Hey, Dr. Francis. It's me." He jumps up in his seat and looks all around. "I'm sitting on your right side," you continue. "I drank one of the vials." His eyes are big when he looks in your direction, like he can't believe you didn't destroy the vials like he told you to.

"I'm sorry," you whisper when the captain jumps into his seat and peels out of the driveway behind Ava. "There's a bomb in your house."

There's a loud BOOM behind you. The ground shakes and the van skids wildly. Dr. Francis grunts through the duct tape and thrashes in his seat.

"It's not my fault," the captain shouts back at him. "All you had to do was tell us where the kids are." He shakes his head and puts a phone to his ear when it rings. "What?" he yells into it. "Yeah. Okay." He hangs up and complains, "I can't believe she needs to get gas."

The captain turns his head back to Dr. Francis. "That's why Ava needs you. She can't do anything right on her own." He faces the road again and follows Ava into a gas station. "Don't go anywhere," he jokes as he gets out and joins Ava at a pump.

You peel the duct tape back from Dr. Francis's mouth. "I'm so sorry," you tell him honestly. "Mrs. Francis wants me here to help you."

He nods and says, "It's not your fault. She's going to be okay." You're not sure how that's possible because she was in the house when the bomb exploded.

"You drank from the vial labelled MASK, didn't you?" he continues. You nod. "Simply amazing. I can't see you at all." He looks through the van windows for Ava and the captain. "Neither can they. You need to get out of here before we get to the research facility."

"Why?" you ask. "What's going on?"

He looks around nervously. "I created a universal cure for the military. I thought I could change the world and save millions of lives, but it has side effects."

"What kind of side effects?" you wonder out loud.

"Nothing anyone's ever seen before," he answers. "The side effects act like superhuman powers." He winks in your direction. "Like being invisible. I can't let Ava and the military have access to it. Their intentions are not good."

"One more question," you say. He nods. "Why do they want Kim and Kevin?"

He sighs. "The side effects are much stronger on children."

The side van door opens and the captain sticks his head inside. "How did the duct tape come off your mouth?" he says to Dr. Francis while rolling his eyes at Ava. "Never trust a civilian to do a veteran's job." He reaches in to put the tape back on.

"The doctor's gone crazy," the captain says to Ava as he pushes the duct tape back over Dr. Francis's mouth.

To stay in the van, turn to page 60.

To get out and ask for help, turn to page 88.

YOU CLOSE YOUR EYES AND IMAGINE being back in Dr. Francis's office, surrounded by his computer desk and the table with the bomb on it. Now reopen your eyes.

You're staring at the bomb with red flashing numbers. The display shows 0:17. "Seventeen seconds," you gasp.

You carefully lift the bomb off the table to feel how heavy it is—not very light, maybe twenty pounds. That's heavy enough to sink in a large body of water. Drowning this in the lake that's a mile away or the pond just down the road are the best options.

Hurry! 0:08 is flashing on the bomb!

To throw the bomb in the pond,
Turn to page 62.

To throw the bomb in the lake,
Turn to page 90.

YOU TURN FROM THE DOCTOR and reach for the bomb. It's heavier than you thought it would be, but you'll do whatever it takes to get it out of here and away from everyone.

You rush to the front door with the bomb in your hands. As you run into the yard and down the driveway, you struggle to stuff the bomb under your right arm and against your side.

"Up, up, up," you keep repeating. "This has to work. Fly. Fly!"

Your feet lift off the ground and you're airborne. The bomb almost slips from beneath your arm, but you grab it with both hands and hold it in front of you. This makes it harder to stay in the air but it's the only way you can take the bomb away from here.

The bomb beeps. You look down at the display and see there are only ten seconds left. The lake is the best place you can think of to take this and it isn't far from here, but you're not sure you can make it there in ten seconds. You won't give up though and keep pushing forward.

You whoosh over cars and houses as you push your body to go as fast as it can through the air.

There's the lake! You're going to make it.

The bomb beeps again. There are five seconds left before it explodes. It's slipping from your hands and you're not sure you can hold on to it any longer.

To drop the bomb, turn to page 65.

To keep going to the lake, turn to page 221.

"**HAVE IT YOUR WAY,**" Ava says to you. She turns her attention to the captain. He's back on his feet after you sent him sailing across the room. "Captain, grab the computer and let's go. It should have all the research I need."

"What about the bomb?" you ask. It's down to two minutes now.

She glances at the bomb and shrugs like she's sorry. "It's counting down quickly. You should run." The captain passes her on his way out with the computer in his arms. "Good luck," she calls back as she follows the captain out the front door and closes it.

You rush to Dr. Francis's side and rip the duct tape off his mouth. You work quickly to untie him but you can't because you've never seen these kinds of knots before.

"You've got to get out of here," he pleads. "Save yourself."

"I'm not going anywhere, doctor," you tell him, focusing on the knots. "What did I drink?"

"You weren't supposed to touch the vials," he scolds, "but I'm glad you did. You drank from the one with no label, didn't you?" You nod. "It's never been tested on humans, but I believe it makes you invincible. Nothing can hurt you and it gives you super strength."

"That's awesome," you say, "but right now I wish I could super untie these knots."

"None of that matters," he says. "You need to leave me behind. There's no reason for both of us to be here when the bomb explodes."

You shake your head.

"Look at me," he demands. "When I sent you into the lab, I also notified the police from my computer and they should be here soon. My family—my wife, Kevin, and Kim—are in a safe location. You've done everything you can and none of this is your fault." He nods toward the bomb. "Look! Get out of here!"

You look back at the bomb and see there are only ten seconds left before it goes kaboom. The doctor is still talking, but you can't hear anything he says. All you can think about is that you are invincible. He said nothing can hurt you.

Five seconds…

It's your last chance to decide if you're going to rush out of the house and leave the doctor behind or if you're going to cover the bomb with your body, believing it cannot hurt you, and it can save the doctor.

To leave the doctor behind,
turn to page 55.

To cover the bomb with your body,
turn to page 66.

YOU OPEN THE FRONT passenger door of the sports car and step inside. "Thank goodness you're okay," Mrs. Francis says from the back seat.

"Where's our dad?" Kevin asks.

You close your door and turn to face them, unsure of what to say. Kim starts crying as soon as she sees the worry on your face.

Ava opens the driver's door and jumps inside before you can say anything. "Hold on tight," she says frantically. She starts the car and barrels out of the driveway. The van is right behind you.

You're barely on the road when the ground shakes and the car rattles. You look behind you and see that the house windows are blown out and black smoke is blowing out of them. Mrs. Francis and your friends are watching with you. Your stomach churns as you realize the bomb has exploded with Dr. Francis inside.

"I should've saved him," you say quietly, thinking about all the ways you could've gotten Dr. Francis out of the house.

"He'll be fine," Ava says as if nothing is wrong.

"How can you say that?" Mrs. Francis shouts at her. "You did this to him." She wraps her arms around Kim and Kevin.

Ava glances at you and winks. "I tied Dr. Francis's hands and feet. Only I didn't tie them tight." You're not sure if she means what you think she means. Did she give Dr. Francis a chance to escape?

"What are you talking about?" you ask.

She sighs and says, "I was Dr. Francis's assistant. I would never hurt him."

Mrs. Francis scoffs. "I've never heard of you."

"No," she says, looking at her from the rearview mirror. "You wouldn't have." She focuses on you. "The captain is not a good man. He will do anything to retrieve the vials you destroyed."

"Why?" you wonder out loud. "What was so important about those vials?" You're not sure you can trust anything she's saying because she's with the captain and appears to be in charge of him.

"Dr. Francis has been working for years to find a universal cure for sickness and disease," Ava says. "He finally found something that works. That's what was in those vials." She shakes her head. "Only it doesn't work the way it's supposed to."

"Then why does the captain care about it?" you ask, pointing to the van behind you.

The gas light on the car's dashboard lights up bright orange. "Hang on a second." She pulls out her cell phone and presses a button on it. "I've got to pull into the next gas station," she says into the receiver. "I know. There's no way I can get there without gas. Okay." She puts the phone in her lap. "What were we talking about?"

"A cure that doesn't work right," you remind her.

"Oh, yeah," she says. "Dr. Francis tested it on old mice and was successful. Mice who couldn't walk could suddenly run.

Some became faster. Some became stronger. It's the most amazing thing I've ever seen." You nod as you remember the mouse in Dr. Francis's office running faster than possible. "It doesn't work the same way on humans."

"If it doesn't work on humans then why does anyone care?" you point out.

Ava pulls the car into a gas station and up to a pump. She turns the car off and puts the keys in her pocket. "I didn't say it doesn't work on humans. I said it doesn't work the same way." She opens her door and turns to you. "It works best on children."

"Wait," you say before she steps out. "You're saying children become faster and stronger than any other humans?"

"And other abilities," she says. "You would probably call them metahumans or superhumans." She looks back to Kim, Kevin, and Mrs. Francis. "I don't know what the captain has planned for you, but I fear he will make me use you as test subjects. I'm going to do everything I can to protect you."

"That's not so bad," Kevin says. "I'd like to be faster and stronger."

Ava puts one foot out the door. "Test subjects are locked away and never allowed to see the light of day again."

Kevin sinks back into his seat. "Oh. Never mind then."

"I'll be back in a few minutes." Ava exits the car and closes her door.

"Listen to me," Mrs. Francis whispers from behind you. "I don't trust her. You're the only one who can help us."

"How?" you ask.

"Your door was never locked." You realize she's right. In all the confusion of rushing out of the yard before the bomb exploded, Ava didn't lock you in. "The store is full of people and I saw a woman wearing a security uniform."

You look to your right at the gas station store. There are maybe a dozen people inside. You see the woman with the security uniform. Maybe she can help and even call for backup.

If you run for the store and get caught then you may be severely punished. But if you don't run and get help, you and your friends may become test subjects locked away forever.

Ava is done pumping gas and about to get back into the car. What do you do?

To run into the store, turn to page 57.

To stay in the car, turn to page 70.

MRS. FRANCIS STARES in your direction as you open her car's passenger door and sit down inside.

"I feel the same way," you reply as you close the door.

She drives down the driveway and out of the yard at full speed. A fire truck and an ambulance pass from the opposite direction with lights flashing and sirens roaring. "I wonder what your family would say about this," she muses.

"Don't worry," you say. "I don't think anyone will believe any of this. I'm not sure I do."

She nods. "That's fair." The gas light flashes on the car. "He never fills up the gas tank," she mumbles angrily while pounding a fist on the steering wheel. She takes a deep breath and looks toward you. "You're still in the front seat, right?"

"Yes, ma'am," you confirm. "What's going to happen to me?"

Her face softens. "My husband is a brilliant man. I'm not supposed to know this but he created a universal cure for most sicknesses and diseases. It his side effects that act a lot like superpowers."

"Like being invisible," you whisper.

"He and Ava were partners in a military research project to find treatments and cures for soldiers," she explains. "Once he found the side effects to his latest discovery, he kept it away from Ava and the military, knowing they would use it the wrong way."

You're not sure what the wrong way is but can guess it involves giving superpowers to the military. Mrs. Francis pulls the car into a gas station and says, "I'll be back in a minute." She gets out and pumps gas into the car.

You see a security guard in the gas station store and think about getting her attention. You'll do everything you can to help Mrs. Francis, but it may be impossible to help Dr. Francis without help.

To stay in the car and wait, turn to page 96.

To go into the store and ask for help, turn to page 112.

YOU TURN AWAY from Dr. Francis and run down his driveway as fast as you can. You've got to take off into the sky before you reach the mailbox at the end because you're running so fast that if you don't take off, you'll trip over your feet and your head will crash and slide across the pavement like a bowling ball.

Here comes the mailbox…

This has to work! It has to!

Okay, here we go…

Now jump!

You did it! You're flying!

Watch out for that tree. Turn to your right. Not that right—your other right. Okay, that's better.

Brush those leaves out of your hair. The wind feels awesome as it blows past you, like driving a go-cart a hundred miles an hour. Get that gnat out of your teeth.

It's hard to fly straight but you're getting it. Go a little higher so you can see all of the houses and cars below you. You can do this. Find that green, brown, and gray camouflaged military van and yellow sports car.

Up ahead, you see them. Focus on flying straight. Don't fly too low because you don't want to scare other people while they're driving.

You can see clearly from here that there's no one in the van except for the captain. This is great! You can't rule out that Kim, Kevin, and Mrs. Francis aren't in the car yet though. You have to keep going.

You're getting closer, but what are you going to do when you get there? You can't stay in the air forever because Dr. Francis thinks your ability to fly may only last thirty minutes. At least ten of those have already passed. You better land soon.

The top of the van is big enough for you to land on safely, like a helicopter pad. You've got to do it carefully and quietly so the captain doesn't know you're there. Ease down from the air as lightly as you can over the speeding van. It looks like you'll be able to land as quietly as a bird.

54

Nope!

You crash onto the roof like an asteroid, making more noise than an erupting volcano. The van swerves to the right and then the left, trying to make whatever landed on the roof (you) fall off. You lie down flat and hold on as tight as you can.

The van is finally going straight again. The captain will get out soon to see what's up here. You've got to fly away before he can do that.

It's harder and harder to hold on to the van as it zips through traffic. You try to get to your feet and fly away, but you're too weak now. You've got to do something before you fall off.

There, on the right side of the road, old boxes are piled up by businesses and large dumpsters are wide open. You can jump off and land in one of those. You're not sure how safe it is but it's got to be far safer than landing in the street.

Maybe if you hold on a little longer you can find out if Mrs. Francis and your friends are in the car and where they're being taken. You'll probably lose that chance forever if you let go.

To stay on top of the van, turn to page 79.

To let go of the van, turn to page 135.

YOU DON'T WANT TO LEAVE the doctor behind, but it's your only chance to make it out of here. You jump up and run for your life toward the front door.

The bomb explodes as soon as your right foot is out the door, throwing you face down onto the porch while glass from the windows shatters all around you.

You get back up and face the house. You're surrounded by smoke and can't see anything inside. "Doctor!" you shout, hoping he'll answer.

Neighbors run out of their homes and pull you back. They try to comfort you and make sure you're okay. You fight to go back inside but they won't let you because it's too dangerous.

A police car and a fire truck arrive. After securing the area and making you stand back, the firefighters enter the house and search for any survivors.

"What's your name?" an officer asks you. You tell him who you are and that you live across the street. "Why were you in this house? Neighbors say you ran out when it exploded."

You explain that your family is gone for a weekend trip and you're staying here for a birthday party with your friends.

"Where are your friends?"

You shrug and say, "I don't know, but Dr. Francis said they're safe."

"Let me make sure I understand," he says as a female f joins him. "You don't live here and a bomb went off when you left the house. No one is able to verify anything other than that?"

"My family can but they're visiting a part of Virginia where their cell phones don't work because of a huge telescope."

A firefighter comes out of the house and approaches the officers while they whisper to each. "There are no bodies inside," he reports. "The kid was the only person in there."

Dr. Francis got out and survived somehow! Maybe another secret room you don't know about. But how did he get untied? It doesn't matter. He's out there somewhere, alive.

"You need to come with us," the female officer says. You can see that she doesn't believe anything you've said. Dr. Francis can vouch for you but no one knows where he is.

"I didn't tell you everything," you admit. You tell them how you were supposed to destroy the vials in a secret lab to keep them from Ava but you drank one of them and now you're strong and invincible.

The female officer grabs her walkie talkie and says a bunch of numbers, some kind of code. She leads you to her car and you try to prove your strength by bashing a fist on the hood. Your fist bounces back and it hurts. Where did your strength go?

She puts you into the back of her car. Then she says to whoever's on the other end of the walkie talkie, "Yeah, must be a full moon tonight."

>>time travel back to page 45<<
THE END

YOU THROW THE DOOR OPEN and rush for the store. You've got to get inside before the captain can stop you because you're sure this is your only chance to save yourself and get help for your friends.

"Hey!" the captain shouts from the van. You don't turn to face him because it will only slow you down.

You reach the store's front entrance and yank the glass door open. Cool air blows across your face and the smell of fresh hot dogs fills your nostrils. The security guard isn't up front and you don't see her anywhere in the store. You shout the only word you can think of. "Help!"

A cashier with a ring in her eyebrow stares at you from behind the counter and two customers approach you. "Are you okay?" one man asks.

"Are you hurt?" the other asks.

You look behind you and through the glass doors to see if the captain is close. He's standing by the pumps and arguing with Ava, waving his hands in the air and pointing at the store.

"Where's the security guard?" you ask the customers around you. Your face feels like it's on fire from running and you probably look like a crazy person with your chest heaving up and down.

"In the bathroom," the cashier calls out, nodding to the back of the store.

"Call 911," you tell her as you pass by and navigate to the back. "My friends outside have been kidnapped."

The first door you find in the back has an image of a man

on it and the door after it has an image of a woman. You knock vigorously on the second door.

"Give me a minute!" the woman inside shouts. "I had tacos for lunch."

"I need your help!" you cry. "My friends have been kidnapped and they're outside in a sports car."

"What?" she says. "Is this a joke?"

"Please," you say, desperate for the guard to believe you. "My friends and their mom are in trouble. Someone has to save them."

A toilet paper roll spins on the other side of the door and a few sheets are ripped off in quick succession before the toilet flushes. The restroom door opens and a large woman in a uniform with a shiny badge steps out.

"Show me," she says with a hand on her holster.

You lead her through the store as quickly as you can. "A woman with red hair has them in her car. A man in a military uniform is helping her, and he's in a van behind the car."

"I called the cops," the cashier says as you pass the register. "They should be here in a few minutes."

You strain to see the sports car and military van as you approach the glass doors. There's a man in greasy overalls blocking your view.

"Move away from the door," the guard orders. The man apologizes and steps aside.

The sports car and dark military van are gone. You push the exit door open and step outside with the security guard by your side. You look right and left to see if the vehicles are anywhere on the road. They're not. You have no idea how to find them and neither will the police.

You wish you had stayed in the car with Kim, Kevin, and Mrs. Francis. Maybe you could have saved them. Now they're going to become test subjects and locked away forever.

>>time travel back to page 49<<
THE END

YOU SIT BACK in your seat and stay quiet because you're committed to staying with the doctor to help him in any way you can. If the world really is in danger, you'll do everything in your power to save it.

The captain gets back into the van and asks:

He turns on the radio and plays a Katy Perry song called "Roar." It's cool and all but totally weird when the captain sings along in a high-pitched voice.

"Mrs. Francis said Kim and Kevin will be okay," you whisper to Dr. Francis. "Is that possible if the house blew up?"

He blinks his eyes and nods.

"I don't know about you but I'm hungry," the captain says. "I feel like a burger. Sound good? Kind of like a last supper for you." The doctor still doesn't move.

The captain picks up his phone and dials a number. "We're getting burgers," he says into the receiver. "Yes, we are. You're not the one in charge—I am." He shuts his phone off and tosses it on the seat next to him. "I don't know how you ever worked with her," he says back Dr. Francis. He pulls into a burger joint and drives up to the drive-thru speaker.

"Yeah," he says into the speaker, "let me have five super duper extra-large burger meals." He pulls forward, grabs the meals at the second window, and parks the van in the lot.

"No one makes burgers like my mama, but this will work," the captain says as he digs through the bag. "Wait a minute. Wait … a … minute. There are only four burgers in here. No way. No stinking way." He looks back at the drive-thru line and sees it wraps around the building. "I've got to go inside and fix this. Don't go anywhere." He jumps out of the van, locks it, and walks to the restaurant with a scowl on his face.

You rip the duct tape off Dr. Francis's mouth again and realize this may be the only chance to get him out of here.

To untie the doctor and run away, turn to page 102.

To stay in the van, turn to page 119.

YOU SLAM YOUR EYES SHUT and imagine the pond down the road that's covered in slimy green scum and smells like dead fish. Reopen your eyes.

The red numbers flash 0:02. Throw it! Throw the bomb!

Nice toss. Now turn around and run for your life!

Thunder rumbles behind you and water shoots up into the air like an erupting volcano. You dive to the ground and cover your head as the water pushes you forward like an angry bully.

An old shoe lands next to your face. It's not yours. Weird. You stand up and look back at the huge hole left where the pond water was seconds ago. Now close your eyes and teleport back to your friends.

Kevin is staring at you with an odd expression on his face. "Why are you wet?"

Kim pinches her nose closed with two fingers. "And why do you smell like fish?" You explain what happened with the bomb at the pond.

"You may have saved us," Mrs. Francis says. "That was brave, but please don't do that again. I would never forgive myself if something happened to you."

She grabs some clothes and tosses them to you. "You can change in the back. There's a small bathroom." You thank her and change quickly.

"Have a seat," Mrs. Francis tells you when you come back into the main room. "You too," she says to her kids. You, Kevin, and Kim sit next to each other on one cot and face her on the next cot. "Your father researches new ways to treat sicknesses in the military," she tells your friends. She turns her attention to you. "He discovered something that can give you superpowers."

"That's not medicine," Kevin says. "It's superhero serum."

"Be quiet," Kim urges him.

He pokes her and replies, "You be quiet."

"Okay," Mrs. Francis says, "that's enough." Kim crosses her arms and Kevin shakes his head. "The superpowers are a temporary side effect of medicine he created. It boosts the immune system to unheard of levels that can fight most sicknesses and diseases."

"How long will I be able to teleport?" you ask.

She shrugs and says, "The medicine is in testing phases with mice. The superpowers can last for weeks on them. With someone your size, I suppose it will be much shorter."

"Wait," Ki, says, holding up a hand. "There's more than one superpower?" She turns to you. "What else can you do?" You shrug because you're not sure you can do anything else.

"Your father was able to separate the side effects for testing," Mrs. Francis explains to Kim. "He assigned different colors to different side effects."

"Mine was orange," you volunteer.

She nods. "My husband's assistant discovered he was hiding this research; that he brought it to his lab here." She stands and stretches. "She's angry that he kept it from her and the military."

"And now she's taken him," you say. "There's something else. I heard her tell the captain that she has experiments to run on the children. What children?"

"I don't know," Mrs. Francis admits. "I'm glad you're all safe." Kevin nods vigorously.

Maybe you're safe but Dr. Francis and other children aren't. Your ability to teleport is temporary so you have a limited time to use it. You remember the moment you saw Ava's yellow sports car and the captain's camouflaged van race away.

You hate to leave your friends behind again, but you've got to save the others while you can.

To teleport to Ava's sports car, turn to page 105.

To teleport to the captain's military van, turn to page 122.

THERE'S NO WAY you can hold on to the bomb any longer because your arms are about to fall off. You make sure you're not over any houses or cars and no one is around then let go.

The bomb lands in the middle of an old dirt road. There's nothing but an abandoned building and old car nearby. No one is around so no one will be hurt. You begin to fly away but stop.

A bus full of passengers turns onto the road and heads straight toward the bomb at full speed. You freak out and try to think fast about what your options are.

You could fly down and stand in the bus's way so it stops but it's going so fast that it may not be able to do so in time. A better option may be to fly away to find your friends and save them.

To stop the bus, turn to page 92.

To save your friends, turn to page 213.

YOU JUMP INTO ACTION and snatch the bomb off the table with both hands and hug it to your chest. You run as fast as you can into the lab, away from the doctor, and dive to the floor with it.

The bomb explodes beneath you.

Your body flies three feet off the floor and crashes back down. You're not hurt though. You feel with your hands over your arms, legs, stomach, neck, and even your head. Everything is still there.

Your shirt, however, is in shreds. It looks like dangling spaghetti noodles in the front.

You head back to Dr. Francis's office, grab the blue towel off the table, and wrap it around your front and back. He stares at you with big eyes, like you're a ghost.

YOU SAVED ME. YOU RISKED YOUR LIFE.

You bend down and take another look at the rope around him. The knots are tricky, but you've got more time to figure them out now.

"I wish I had never discovered these powers," he says. "They've been nothing but trouble. I'm sorry that you're involved with this."

You tell him that there's no need to apologize. All the bad stuff aside, being strong and invincible is awesome. Imagine what you can do with this power. "I can help people."

"I have no doubt that you would," he agrees, smiling. "You just proved that."

You figure out the knots and get his legs untied. Now for his hands…

"I have more work to do on the formulas first," he says. "The vial you drank from was only to test mice with. Given your size, it may only work for thirty minutes." He sighs. "When I've finalized the formula, there will be no more powers."

"What do you mean?" you ask.

"My job is to find and create treatments and cures for sickness and disease," he explains. "I believe I've created something that can strengthen the body's immune system far beyond anything we ever thought possible." He wiggles his legs to shake away some of the numbness. "The problem is that my current formulation has side effects that give anyone superhuman capabilities—especially children."

You finally get his hands untied. There's some blood on the rope from where he tried to wrestle his wrists out of it. He stands and walks around the room until he has feeling throughout his body again.

"What happened to Kim, Kevin, and Mrs. Francis?" you ask him.

"I set up a process years ago with a panic room," he explains. "It's hidden behind the kitchen pantry." He motions for you to follow him to the kitchen and points inside the pantry full of food. "Watch this." He pushes down the top shelf and all of the shelves collapse to the floor. There's a steel door behind the area where the shelves were.

"How is that possible?" you ask. "Where did the food go?"

He chuckles. "There is no food. There never was." He waves a hand over the shelves on the floor and a holographic light appears over his hand. "Everything you saw on the shelves was nothing more than a holographic image."

You're amazed by this, but you have a much bigger question. "Do we just go through the door to get your family, knock on it, or what?"

Dr. Francis shakes his head. "The panic room is set to lock for two hours automatically, no exceptions. No one can go in or out during that time. This is for protection against home invasions and natural disasters."

"But how did they know to go in there?" you wonder out loud.

He points to the lights above you. "The lights flash orange throughout the house with a simple command from my computer." Now you understand the process he uses to protect his family.

"The lights flash orange and they know to hide in the panic room," you mumble. "Genius."

"Maybe," he whispers. "I don't know for sure that my family is in there."

"What do you mean?" you ask, confused.

He looks away from you. "I heard my wife scream. I don't know if they were taken." He clears his throat and walks out of the kitchen and into the living room where you were playing video games less than twenty minutes ago. "I've got to find Ava so I know for sure. I can't just sit here, waiting."

"What should I do?" I ask.

"The police will be here soon," he says. "Tell them what happened with Ava and the bomb—nothing else. No one needs to know about my formulas yet." He pauses and takes a breath. "If I don't make it back before the panic room door opens, let my family know that I'm okay."

You think it may be a better idea if you go with him because you're strong and invincible, which will help if there's danger. He's not sure but is okay with it.

To stay in the house, turn to page 94.

To go with Dr. Francis, turn to page 109.

YOU STAY IN THE CAR with Kim, Kevin, and Mrs. Francis because it feels like the right thing to do. But there's a knot in your stomach.

"Gas prices are crazy," Ava says as she gets back into the car. She reaches across the dashboard and blasts the air conditioning at full speed. "That's better."

No one responds to her as the sports car eases back onto the highway. You keep trying to think of ways to escape with your friends. It seems impossible with the van behind you.

"No one was supposed to get hurt," Ava says quietly. "I didn't know you would be taken."

"You're a bad person," Kim says from the back.

Ava sighs and says, "We're going to be at the research facility in a few hours. I need all of you to stay with me when we get there." She looks up at the rearview mirror and the van behind you. "He's going to try to separate all of you. I'll do whatever I can to keep that from happening." She winks at you. "I have a plan to get you out."

The rest of the trip is silent. The car slows down and your stomach churns because you know you're almost there, a place no one should have to go to. You look back at Mrs. Francis and Kim and Kevin. Their faces look the same way Dr. Francis's did when you walked into his office and saw the mouse running faster than any mouse is supposed to.

Ava drives down a hidden road and stops at a security booth in front of a large metal gate. A man in a military uniform steps out of the booth, looks at everyone in the car, then nods at Ava and presses a button that opens the gate.

Now the car is in front of a large white warehouse without any words on it. Ava nods at you and says, "Here we go. Stay by my side. I won't let anything happen to you or your friends." She turns and faces the family. "I'm going to get all of you out of here."

Your door is suddenly yanked open. The captain is standing there and says, "Get out." Kim screams as he leads you away to the facility.

The captain opens the facility's front door and prods you down a long marble hallway. There are rooms with large glass windows on each side that have metal beds. Young people in the rooms bang on the glass as you pass them, like they want you to get them out.

You're finally tossed into one of the rooms and thrown onto a medical bed that's sitting in an upright position. The captain straps you down so you can't move.

An old man in a lab coat walks in. He's holding a syringe in one hand and squirts a stream of liquid up into the air from it. The captain motions for him to work on you.

You close your eyes and hope this doesn't hurt. You don't know what's happening to your friends. You don't know if they're going to be okay. All you know is you're never getting out of here and it's all your fault.

Ava steps into the room and says, "Stop." The man in the lab coat backs up. Ava walks past him and the captain and stands in front of you. "Foolish child," she says. I could never let you go. You're the perfect age and size for what we need."

You don't know what she's talking about. "I should never have trusted you. Where are my friends?"

She laughs. "I don't have much use for them." She nods at the man in the lab coat for him to come back.

"You lied about everything," you remind her. "I can't believe anything you say."

She shrugs and stands back as the man in the lab coat brings the syringe close to your arm. "Most of what I said was true. Dr. Francis created a cure that has side effects that give superpowers to kids like you."

The man in the lab coat jabs you with his needle and leaves the room. "In just a minute you won't remember any of this," Ava says. "You will be completely reprogrammed. "We are creating an army of children with superpowers to help us take over the world. You will be the most feared child in history." She walks away slowly. "Thank you for volunteering."

The room is growing dark. Your arms feel heavy. You could've drunk from a vial. You could've selected a superpower. If only you could start all over again then you could.................................

>>time travel back to page 49<<
THE END

YOU CLOSE THE FRONT DOOR while Mrs. Francis gets into her car and drives away. A fire truck and an ambulance race into the driveway just as she disappears. You step outside to tell them what happened but remember they can't see you.

"Search the house!" one firefighter yells to the others. "Make sure no one is inside." Two firefighters enter the house. As you watch them, you notice smoke shooting up into the sky from the back of the house.

A police car pulls into the driveway and two officers get out. One is a tall man and the other is a short woman. "What happened here?" the tall officer asks.

"Some kind of explosion," the firefighter giving orders explains. "I don't think anyone's inside, but we're making sure of it."

"Do you live here?" the short officer asks you. You look around to see who she's talking to because you're invisible but she's looking directly into your eyes.

"Me?" you ask. "You can see me?"

Her eyes narrow. "Yeah, do you live here?" she repeats. You remember Mrs. Francis said you wouldn't be invisible forever and shake your head. "Did you see what happened?"

You tell her that you live across the street and two people broke into the house. They had a bomb with them. She pulls out a notepad and starts writing.

"What did they look like?" she prompts.

"There was a woman with long red hair," you explain, "and a really big man wearing a military uniform."

"Where were you?" she asks, still writing.

"I was invisible," you say without thinking. She closes her notebook and shakes her head at her partner. "My friends are inside," you continue. "They're in a safe room."

"How many?" the firefighter asks.

"Two," you say. "Kim and Kevin. Today's their birthday."

The firefighter jerks his walkie talkie to his face and shouts, "Two inside! Two kids! Get them out!" A voice responds that the search is complete. There is no one inside.

"Where are your parents?" the tall officer asks you with a frown.

"My family is out of town for the weekend," you explain. "There's no way to reach them."

"I think we need to talk some more at the station," he says, motioning to the police car. You reluctantly go with the officers downtown.

By the time your family comes for you, the Francises are gone and there's a For Sale sign in their front yard. You'll never know why they were attacked. You'll never know what happened to Kim, Kevin, and their parents.

>>time travel back to page 26<<
THE END

YOU APPROACH THE TWO POLICE OFFICERS on scene to tell them what happened. While the lady officer is short, the man officer is tall and skinny. "I saw everything," you admit.

They take you aside and ask for your story. You tell them about Ava, the captain, and the bomb. You also explain there's a panic room in the house and the family is inside.

The officers pull a firefighter aside and advise him of the panic room. The firefighter quickly puts together a team to search for it.

You're worried the officers won't believe anything you say about the secret lab or vials. The only way to make them believe is to teleport right in front of them. They look at each other funny when you say you're going to do this.

You close your eyes and picture the dirty, smelly clothes on your bedroom floor but stop when you hear Kim and Kevin call out your name. The firefighters lead them outside with Mrs. Francis.

"We made it," Kim says as she hugs you.

"Do you know this kid?" the lady officer asks Mrs. Francis while nodding at you. She lowers her voice and coughs. "Did you know the kid can teleport?" The man officer chuckles.

Mrs. Francis shrugs and says you have a wild imagination that the family loves. She rubs your head. She explains that you're staying with her kids while your family is away for the weekend.

"My home was robbed and my husband is missing," she says. The officers take her aside and ask her more questions.

"Glad you told them we were in there," Kevin says to you. "I was afraid we'd have to eat beef jerky and canned chicken for a few months."

"I knew we could count on you," Kim adds. "I hope we can find our dad soon."

"We'll figure it out," you assure them, though you don't know if that's true or not. The only thing you know for sure is that they're your friends and you'll do whatever you can to help.

Mrs. Francis rejoins you and says, "We'll get a hotel room until this is sorted out." She looks over the damaged house and sighs. "There's a lot to explain but there's somewhere I have to go right now. It can't wait."

"What?" Kevin asks. "What about us?"

"Mom, what's going on?" Kim asks. "Don't leave us alone."

"I won't be gone very long," Mrs. Francis promises. She turns to you. "Can they stay with you until I get back?"

You're not sure what could be more important than being with her family right now ... unless ... maybe she knows where Dr. Francis is. You agree to let Kim and Kevin come to your house.

"That was crazy," Kevin says when you're back in your house. "Orange lights flashed throughout our house. It's our dad's system to let us know to hide in extreme danger."

"We went into the safe room like we practiced a million times," Kim adds. "But this time it was for real. And then you appeared from thin air."

You tell them everything that happened since you first stepped into their dad's office, starting with the mouse running superfast in the wheel. They're amazed by what their dad has accomplished.

"So that's why I keep getting new mice," Kim realizes.

"Our dad controlled so much from his computer," Kevin says. "I wish it wasn't destroyed in the blast. Maybe it could've helped us find him."

"Maybe it still can," Kim says excitedly. "Do you have a computer?" she asks you. You nod and take her to it. She immediately gets on the internet. "Dad let me use his computer once to do my homework."

"What?" Kevin asks. "He let you in his office?"

"He likes me more," she replies, smiling.

"Whatever, Daddy's girl," he says.

"He never let me see his files," Kim says to you, "but I know a thing or two about computers." She goes to a website that says something about cloud storage. "Our dad would definitely save everything in the clouds." You remember learning about that in school. It's basically putting the information from your computer onto another computer that's secure on the internet so you can access it from anywhere.

"Daddy uses the same username for everything, but I don't

know what the password is," she says, trying to think what he would use.

"Try: Pizza," Kevin offers.

"That's brilliant," Kim replies, rolling her eyes.

"Try today's date," you say, remembering how you guessed it right in Dr. Francis's office. "Use two numbers for the month, two numbers for the day of the month, and four numbers for the year."

Kevin scoffs. "Why? Of all the dates in the year, why would it be today?"

"Because it's your birthday," you say, nudging Kim to put it in. "His password is your birthday."

Kim shrugs and puts in the password. "It works!" she exclaims.

Three familiar folders stare back at you. They're named LAB, WORK, and PANIC. You already know PANIC leads to the panic room. Two choices are left.

To tell Kim to open LAB, turn to page 98.

To tell Kim to open WORK, turn to page 114.

YOUR ARMS ARE TIRED and hurting from holding onto the van's roof for so long but you refuse to let go. You're glad you didn't because the van is slowing down and entering a gas station.

As soon as it stops, you stand to your feet so you can try to fly away and hide. But how can you do it without running first? What was it you said to yourself back in the lab so you could fly down from the ceiling?

Oh, yeah! You said, "Down, down, down." Try the opposite fast. The driver's door is opening on the truck. The captain is stepping out.

You close your eyes and say, "Up, up, up." Your body feels weightless again. You reopen your eyes and dart toward the gas station store entrance just in time.

You come down for a soft landing. It's got to go better than how you crashed onto the van's roof. Slowly, slowly, carefully...

Look out for that garbage can! You crash into it and trash flies up into the air and all over the parking lot.

Stand up tall and straighten out your clothes. Hopefully no one saw you. Flying may freak them out but this is embarrassing. There's a rotten banana peel on top of your head. Toss it off, clear your throat, and focus on the van and sports car.

The captain is looking over the roof of his van. You left a large dent in it.

Ava's car is in front of him and next to a gas pump. She

steps out and begins to fill the car up with gas. You strain to see through the car windows so you can tell if your friends and Mrs. Francis are in there. It's hard to tell for sure from this distance because the windows are tinted.

You turn toward the captain and see he's staring at you with a frown. You look down at your toes and whistle. Does the captain know you were on top of his van? You're having a hard time breathing.

"Why were you driving like a madman?" Ava calls out to the captain while her car tank fills up.

"Come take a look at this," he says, nodding to the van roof. She sighs and walks over to him. They're on the opposite side of the van now. You can't see them and they can't see you.

A car pulls up next to you and a young man in jeans and a baseball jersey gets out. He's holding a cell phone up to his ear. "I'm getting milk," he says into it. "Do we need anything else?"

You promised to let Dr. Francis and the police know when you found his wife and children. Maybe you should ask this man if you can make a call on his phone. But Ava and the captain are distracted right now. It may be your only chance to get Kim, Kevin, and Mrs. Francis out of the car safely. Tough choice. What do you do?

To get the family out of the car, turn to page 100.

To ask the young man for his cell phone, turn to page 152.

YOU STEP OUT OF THE CAR, close the door, and head for the store entrance. A man in front of you is on his cell phone and asking the other person if they need anything from inside. He opens the entrance door and lets you in first.

You look around the store but don't see the security guard anywhere. A stock worker in the back is holding a rickety ladder for another worker changing a light bulb way up high.

"Have you seen the security guard?" you ask the man holding the ladder. He looks over at you then points to the restrooms.

"I saw her headed that way," he says. "I told her not to eat the tacos, but she wouldn't listen." He takes his hands off the ladder and puts them in the air like he can't understand why she ate them.

The ladder wobbles then tumbles over the grocery shelves. The man way up top yells in distress as his body crashes toward the floor.

You rush beneath him and hold out your arms. He lands safely in them, bewildered.

"You saved my life," he says as you help him to his feet.

"How'd you do that?" the man who was holding the ladder asks. "It doesn't seem possible."

You don't have time to talk because Ava told you to come right back. "I need the security guard," you say, walking away toward the restroom.

There she is, waiting outside the restroom, dancing from one foot to the other. She's wearing a black uniform. "C'mon," she whispers to whoever's in there. "C'mon, c'mon, c'mon. Hurry up."

You're not sure what to say to her. All you know is you need help and she's your best hope at the moment. "Excuse me," you say to her.

She turns and looks at you while holding her stomach. She's got a shiny badge and a nametag that says Shannon. "Yeah?" she grunts like she's in pain.

You explain what Ava has done and that she's outside. "You're the only one who can help."

Shannon stops hopping from foot to foot. "What?" The toilet flushes in the restroom and a kid walks out. "Look, stay right here and I'll call 911 while I'm... Just don't go anywhere." She rushes into the restroom and closes the door.

"There's not enough time!" you shout at the door. You can't wait for the police because Ava told you to come right back. If you don't go now, bad things are going to happen. "She's going to hurt him."

Shannon opens the door and stares at you with a grimace on her face. "This better not be a game." Her face is red as she marches past you to the front of the store. "Show me."

You stay back so Ava can't see you through the glass doors but point toward the parking space you were in. The yellow sports car is gone. "I took too long," you whisper.

"Not funny!" the security guard shouts at you as she rushes back to the restroom. "I'm gonna have to change my underwear!"

You step out of the store and look over the parking lot. Ava and the sports car are long gone. She must have seen you talking with the store clerk or Shannon and figured you were turning her in.

You feel sick. Ava said she would tell the captain to restart the bomb. You go back inside and call the police, but you don't know what's happened to your friends or even if you'll ever see them again.

>>time travel back to page 34<<
THE END

YOU STAY IN THE CAR with Ava and tell her you don't have to go to the restroom anymore. You can't risk her turning the bomb back on.

"No one is supposed to get hurt," Ava says as she drives out of the gas station and back onto the road. "When we get to the research facility, I'll do everything I can to protect you." You're not sure if you can believe a single word she's saying. "I'm as much of a prisoner as you."

There's nothing but silence for the longest time and Ava turns the car radio on. It's playing a boring talk show with news breaks. She finally turns down a hidden dirt road and into the woods. It leads to a guard shack.

Ava rolls down her window when a guard in a military uniform steps out of the shack and looks over the car. "Beautiful day," Ava says.

"Yep," he answers. You try to get his attention but he ignores you. A metal gate opens up in front of the car. "Go on, more are coming."

Ava rolls her window up and winks at you. "Everything's going to be okay." She drives forward and now you're staring at a large white warehouse. This must be the research facility. She stops and says, "I'm sorry."

The passenger door next to you opens and a large body looms over you. It's the captain! "Get out," he orders you. How did he get here?

Ava nods at you as you step out of the car. "Where's Dr. Francis?" you ask the captain, confused. He ignores you and marches toward the warehouse, expecting you to follow. He stops at the front door, opens it, and motions for you to get inside.

You look back at Ava's car, wondering if she really will do everything she can to protect you. You doubt it but you've already come this far and you keep pushing forward to make sure the doctor is safe.

The air inside the warehouse blows into your face and is as cold as a freezer. You hug your arms to your chest to stay warm because you're already shivering. A long marble hallway is in front of you. As you follow it, you see rooms with large glass windows on both sides of the hallway. They look like hospital rooms with metal medical beds.

The captain puts you in one of the rooms and laughs. He stands outside the doorway, swipes a security keycard over the door and it closes, sealing you inside.

Now he's holding up what looks like a TV remote control and waving it at you. His mouths the word, "Boom." You realize this is a remote detonator to the bomb.

You sit on the cold metal medical bed. You can't help but feel like you should have done things differently.

The room door opens again and an old man in a lab coat is standing there. He's got a syringe in his hand and squirts liquid up into the air from it. "Stay still," he says, "and this won't hurt."

To take the shot,
turn to page 101.

To try to escape,
turn to page 117.

YOU GET OUT OF THE VAN through the front passenger door and close it quietly so you don't draw any attention. Ava and the captain are standing by her car and arguing while gas pumps into it. You walk calmly to the gas station store and open the entrance door.

It smells like hot dogs in here. There's a cashier behind the counter with long brown hair and a pierced eyebrow. Two workers are carrying a ladder from the back. You notice a phone behind the cashier's counter. If anyone can help, it's the police. You just have to call them.

"Excuse me," you say to the cashier as you approach her. She looks up from a crossword puzzle and searches the area around her then shrugs. You keep forgetting that no one can see you.

You reach around the cashier and grab the phone while she's distracted. You walk to an aisle where there are no workers or customers and dial 911.

"911 … please hold … an operator will be right with you," plays an automated message.

You walk around the store while waiting and gaze out the front window. Ava is getting back into her car. The captain is heading back to his van.

"No … no, no, no," you say in frustration. You set the phone down on a magazine rack and race to get outside and back into the van.

"911," you hear an operator say from the phone. "What's your emergency?" Finally!

"There it is," the cashier says as she walks up to the magazine rack and swipes the phone. She puts it to her ear and says, "Hello? Yeah, there's no emergency here. Sorry." She disconnects the phone and walks back behind the counter mumbling, "Kids playing pranks."

You're back outside just as the van gets onto the highway and disappears in traffic. There's nothing you can do to help now. You have no idea where the van is going. You're never going to see Dr. Francis again. You wish you had stayed in the van.

>>time travel back to page 40<<
THE END

YOU CLOSE YOUR EYES AND IMAGINE the lake with swans and ducks and the sidewalk that wraps around it. Now open your eyes.

You're standing in the lake's shallow water. The red numbers on the bomb flash 0:03.

Throw it! Throw the bomb now!

Nice toss. Now turn around and run for your life! Go! Go! Go!

The ground rumbles around you and water jets into the air like an erupting geyser. You dive to the ground as a ton of water crashes on and around you. Fish are flopping wildly around your body.

"What are you doing?" an old man in a golf cart shouts as he drives to your side. He stops the cart as you get up and face him. "Blast fishing is illegal. And you could've gotten hurt." He waves down a police car that's parked by the sidewalk.

"What's going on here?" a tall officer asks as he approaches you.

"This kid is blast fishing with dynamite," the old golfer accuses you. A flopping fish lands on his shoe and he kicks it back into the lake.

"It wasn't dynamite," you assure the officer. "It was a bomb I had to save my friends from."

"A bomb?" the officer asks. "Why don't you come with me so you can explain everything?" He's got a hand on his holster.

"I can prove I had nothing to do with it," you say. "You can ask Mrs. Francis."

"How can I contact her?"

"You can't right now," you tell him. "She's in a safe room and won't be able to come out for at least another hour."

"A safe room?" the old golfer asks. "Isn't that like a bomb shelter?"

The officer holds up a hand to the golfer and says, "Sir, I need you to step aside while I handle this." He points to the sidewalk. "Stand over there, please." The golfer grunts and walks off. The officer turns his attention back to you. "Let's talk about this downtown."

"I need to teleport back to them," you say without thinking. You wish you hadn't said that because it sounds crazy.

"Let's teleport to the police station and talk about it," the officer says. He puts you in the back of his car.

You try to teleport away but the power doesn't work anymore. You have no idea what the Francises' phone number is and you can't reach your family for the weekend. You hope your friends get out of the safe room without any trouble and you hope Dr. Francis is okay.

You don't tell the officers anything else because they already think you're psycho and they have a psychiatrist standing by. Your family comes for you eventually, but Dr. Francis is never found again.

>>time travel back to page 41<<
THE END

YOU FLY DOWN AT LIGHTNING SPEED and land on the dirt road on one knee, balancing yourself with one hand on the ground. You stand up quickly and hold out a hand for the bus to stop.

The driver slams on the brakes and the bus skids wildly toward you, unable to get traction in the dirt. You close your eyes as gravel flies around you and brakes squeal in your ears.

You reopen your eyes and see the bus stopped inches from your face. The bomb screeches from six feet behind you. Time is out.

You dart beneath the bus for protection as the bomb explodes. The ground shakes and the air all around you is filled with dirt and smoke. You use your hands to feel all over your body to make sure you're not missing any parts. Your head is still here—that's good!

People on the bus above you are screaming. They could be hurt so you scurry from beneath the bus to check on them. You notice right away that the front of the bus is blown apart.

You pound on the bus door until the driver opens it. She is visibly shaken and doesn't say a word.

"Is everyone okay?" you ask the passengers. Some nod and some say yes. They are all teenagers.

"You saved us," a male teen says. He reaches out a hand to you. "My name is Miguel." You shake his hand and tell him your name.

You wonder if you should stick around and explain everything to the police when they come or if you should fly off and find your friends.

To stay and help, turn to page 107.

To fly off and find your friends, turn to page 125.

YOU SIT ON THE COUCH with your hands on your head as Dr. Francis leaves to search for his family. You hope they made it into the panic room and are okay.

Two officers knock on the door, like Dr. Francis said they would. You tell them about the home invasion with Ava and the captain but leave out all details about the vials.

"You don't live here?" the female officer asks.

"I live across the street," you explain.

"Where is the family now?" the male officer asks.

"They're in a panic room behind the kitchen pantry," you tell them. The officers look at each other like they don't believe you. "I can show you," you assure them.

"No need to," the male officer says. "I'll check it out," he tells his partner, and heads to the kitchen.

"Why are you here if you don't live here?" the female officer questions you.

You explain that you're here for a birthday party and spending the weekend with your friends.

"And the towel?" she asks suspiciously. "Why are you wearing a towel? Are you hiding any weapons under there?" You forgot all about the towel you wrapped around you after the bomb ripped your shirt apart.

"Hey," the male officer says as he comes back into the room. "The pantry is full of food." You try to explain the holographic lights, but he stops you. "The office looks like it's been torn apart and equipment is missing. And there's some rope on the floor with blood on it."

The officers put you in handcuffs and haul you out of the house. "We just need to sort a few things out," the female officer says. "You're going away for a long, long time."

<<time travel back to page 69<<
THE END

YOU RELAX AND WAIT for Mrs. Francis to get back into the car. "Ready?" she asks when she's in her seat again and starts the car.

"Yeah," you say.

She pulls out of the gas station and drives for an hour, absently drumming her fingers on the steering wheel the entire time.

You don't answer as she turns off the road and starts driving through an army of trees.

"What are you doing?" you ask, bracing yourself as tight as you can in the seat.

"This is the way," Mrs. Francis says. "At least I think it is. My husband pointed to it once as we drove by." A trail soon appears and leads to a guard shack on her side. A large metal gate is directly ahead.

A guard in a military uniform steps out of the shack and motions for the car to turn around and leave as Mrs. Francis rolls her window down.

"My husband's in there," she tells the guard. "I'm going to get inside one way or another."

"Ma'am," the guard says with a blank face, "this building is for military personnel only. There's no way you're getting in if you don't have the right ID or magic powers."

Magic powers.... You realize you can get into the guard shack without being seen and find a way to open the gate. Mrs. Francis is sure that Dr. Francis is inside.

To stay in the car, turn to page 131.

To go into the guard shack, turn to page 148.

KIM OPENS THE FOLDER named LAB and a video of Dr. Francis in his secret lab begins to play. You grab a chair for Kevin to sit on next to Kim. You stand behind them.

"I'm very excited to show you my newest discovery," Dr. Francis says in the video. He holds up a vial with yellow glowing liquid. "It can boost the immune system to superhuman levels that fight most sicknesses and diseases." He approaches a mouse cage on the same table you were at earlier. "It has peculiar side effects that must be eliminated before human trials can begin." He lets an old mouse drink from the vial. This is all too familiar to you. The mouse gets into the mouse wheel but goes faster and faster until it's only a blur.

"Whoa!" Kevin says.

"How is that possible?" Kim asks with a hand over her mouth.

Dr. Francis places a second mouse cage on the table, next to the first one. He lets that mouse drink from a vial with orange liquid, just like the one you drank. The mouse scratches on the cage glass as it watches the speeding blur in the first cage. A few seconds have passed and the mouse disappears. It reappears in the first cage.

Kim and Kevin both gasp. "That's what happened to you," Kim says. You nod.

"As interesting as they are, I must find a way to eliminate these side effects," Dr. Francis continues. "I've brought this project to my own lab to keep the details from my employer—the military—and my assistant Ava. I fear they will abuse the side effects and use them in a way that does more harm than good." He faces the camera directly. "There is one positive though—the side effects appear to be temporary, based on height and weight. In a human they may only last for thirty minutes, maybe more. Peace be with you." The video ends and all the folders disappear like they were never there.

"Wow," Kevin says. "I know he does medical research, but this is next level."

"Our dad is awesome," Kim adds, nodding her head.

You don't want to scare them but there's something they should know. "I heard Ava say she had experiments to run on children. It's not us, so what children?"

"We've got to tell the police," Kevin insists. He glances out a window. "They're still outside."

You remember how the officers looked at each other funny when you told them you could teleport. They laughed when mentioning it to Mrs. Francis. You also realize that Mrs. Francis probably knows much more than any of you. How many secrets did Dr. Francis tell her? If she knows about everything you just watched then maybe she has an idea where her husband is. And maybe that's where she's going.

To teleport to help Mrs. Francis, turn to page 133.

To talk to the police again, turn to page 150.

THE YOUNG MAN NODS as he passes you and goes into the store. You still haven't seen Ava and the captain and know it's time to save your friends.

You walk quickly toward the sports car, careful not to draw attention to yourself. Your heart is racing. You're almost there.

You reach the car and pull on the back door handle. You can hardly breathe when you hear Ava and the captain arguing close to you. Hopefully you can get the family out in time.

The door won't open. You pull on it over and over again. It's locked somehow from the inside.

"What are you doing?" the captain's booming voice says from behind you.

You gulp and turn to face him. You knew he was big, but this close he looks like Mount Everest. You try to say something, but your mouth won't move.

"This is official police business," Ava says, standing next to the captain. She flashes a badge that looks like it came from a dollar store. "Back away from the car and keep moving."

You're not sure if you can walk away at this point and try to catch back up with them or if you should confront the bad guys and tell them you know what they've done.

To walk away,
turn to page 116.

To confront Ava and the captain,
turn to page 171.

YOU ROLL UP YOUR RIGHT SHIRT SLEEVE and take a deep breath. You've had shots before. Sometimes they hurt. Sometimes they don't. You have no idea what's in the syringe and close your eyes as you get the shot.

"All done," the man in the lab coat says. "You'll want to lie down and get comfortable." He walks out of the room just as Ava comes in.

"You should do what he says," she tells you. "It'll make things easier."

You don't want to lie down but your arms and legs feel heavy, like you can't even lift them. What's going on? You're strong enough to throw a grown man but now you can barely lift a finger.

"I'm sorry it has to be this way," Ava says while you struggle to get your legs up on the bed and lie down. "The power you have could last forever. We can't take that chance. We have to protect ourselves." She pauses and sighs. "You will never move again."

You stare up at the ceiling because you can't turn your head anymore. Your body is frozen in place, just like an ice cube in a freezer. You'll be here forever, experimented on for however long they need you.

You'll never know what happens to Dr. Francis. You'll never know what happens to your friends and Mrs. Francis.

>>time travel back to page 87<<
THE END

YOU TRY TO FIGURE OUT how to untie the knots around Dr. Francis's wrists and arms. The knots are the same as the ones that were around Mrs. Francis. You only have to untie his legs so he can run. Focus. The captain could be back any minute.

"Push the loop away from the knot," Dr. Francis says. "It will loosen the knot and you can pull it apart." He's right. It works! You quickly untie both his wrists and his legs.

You unlock the van and slide open the side door so you and Dr. Francis can escape. You help him get out and run toward the sidewalk next to the highway. You keep looking behind you to make sure the captain isn't coming. There's a city bus stop ahead and a bus is about to stop at it.

"Come on," Dr. Francis says. "That's our ticket out of here." You both watch as the captain approaches his van while you get on the bus. He opens his door and throws his hands up in frustration. Now he's searching under and around every car near the van. He gives up and yells at someone on his phone while the bus drives away with you and the doctor.

"What do we do now?" you ask Dr. Francis.

"I've got a friend a few miles ahead," he says. "He can help us." An old lady missing three front teeth smiles at him and he smiles back.

"I talk to myself too," she says. "And George Washington. And Elvis Presley."

The bus stops near the front of a real estate office and you get off with Dr. Francis. You go inside and he asks for his friend at the front desk.

A tall man with a big cowboy hat and a black mustache appears from a smaller office and tells Dr. Francis to come with him.

"John!" Dr. Francis calls out. They shake hands and smile at each other. You're surprised to hear the doctor tell his friend everything that's happened today when they sit in his office. There's no way any sane person would believe the story.

"We're friends and I believe what you're saying," John says. "Thank you for trusting me." He grins. "Even though you like girly movies."

Dr. Francis clears his throat. "I'm a romantic. No one needs to know that."

"We'll handle this, my friend," John assures him. "We need to get the police and FBI involved. I have some contacts. Give me a few minutes to make some calls." He stands from his desk. "This will be over soon."

He leaves the room to make the calls but you're not sure why he can't just make the calls from here. "How long have you known him?" you ask Dr. Francis.

"Just a few months," he says. "He's a good man. Knows everyone in town. He helped me find the house my family lives in." He leans back in his chair and relaxes.

You watch John through the office window. He's in the lobby, walking in circles, talking intently to someone on his phone. If he has connections to everyone in town, then he's probably the best person to help Dr. Francis.

John shoves the phone into his pocket when another large man enters the building. It's the captain! They shake hands like they're best friends. You close the window blinds as quickly as you can.

"We've got to get out of here," you warn Dr. Francis.

"What are you talking about?" he asks, sitting up straight.

"John is not your friend," you tell him. "He's out there right now with the captain."

"I can't believe this," Dr. Francis says in astonishment. "He's been at my house for dinner many times. My family loves him." His face turns red. "He's been spying on us." Maybe it's all a misunderstanding. Things aren't always what they appear to be.

To wait for John to explain,
Turn to page 138.

To get out of here while you can,
Turn to page 157.

YOU GO TO THE BACK OF THE ROOM and act like you're reading the labels on the stockpile of food. There are cans of fruits and vegetables and candy bars that say MRE on them. Water bottles are all over.

You close your eyes and picture the yellow sports car Ava drove away in. You also picture her face as best you can so you don't end up in someone else's car. You mostly just see her long red hair. Open your eyes again.

You're sitting in the back of Ava's car. The seats are leather. She's in the front, driving down the highway. As you lean over to lay your head down so you can't be seen, you catch a glimpse of the captain's van behind you.

Ava's phone rings up front and she answers it.

She puts the phone down and pulls the car into the next gas station. She steps out after parking at a pump.

You sit up slowly and look around. Ava is behind the car, talking with the captain by his van. They move to the side of the van by the pump and you can't see them anymore. But you do see something far more important.

You see a shadow move in the back of the van. It's got to be Dr. Francis. You don't think it will do you any good to teleport to him right here because the captain is a trained professional, but this may be your only chance to help him.

You look to the gas station store and see a security guard inside. Maybe she can help.

To teleport to the guard for help, turn to page 140.

To stay in the car, turn to page 158.

YOU STAY WITH THE PASSENGERS until the police arrive so you can tell them what happened with the bomb and that your friends may have been taken.

It's been ten minutes and a police car arrives. Two officers get out and step onto the bus. Like you, they make sure everyone is okay before they start asking questions.

"What happened here?" one officer asks. She isn't much taller than you and about the same weight.

The bus driver points to you. "Ask the kid. That's who saved us."

The second officer tells the first one that he'll get your story outside while she interviews the others on the bus. He's taller than six feet and built like a grizzly bear. "Follow me," he says, motioning for you to get off the bus with him.

"It's hot out here," he says when you're outside. "Tell me what happened. Did you see the explosion?"

You explain what happened at Dr. Francis's house and why you had to drop the bomb. He's staring at you like he doesn't believe a word you're saying.

"So ... you can fly?" is all he asks.

The other officer steps off the bus and joins him. "None of them know how this happened," she tells him. "You have anything?"

The grizzly bear looking officer lowers his voice and says, "This kid can fly. And the bomb was dropped in front of the bus by accident."

She raises an eyebrow. "I'll play along. Who dropped the

bomb?" The male officer nods at you. "You did this?" she asks you. "You flew through the air like an airplane and bombed the bus?"

You're not sure what to say. It all sounds crazy now that you're hearing it.

The officers whisper to each other then put you in handcuffs. You're arrested for acts of terrorism and taken away.

>>time travel back to page 93<<
THE END

YOU GRAB A SHIRT from Kim and Kevin's room, change into it, and leave with Dr. Francis. As soon as you get to his car you see the tires are slashed. He grunts and kicks the car.

"Joe owes me a favor," he says and marches to the house on the left. He beats his fist on the door five times and waits.

An old man with a big belly opens the door. "Dr. Francis," he says with a wide smile. "It's a beautiful day. What can I do for you?"

"You can let me borrow your car, Joe."

Joe's smile disappears. "What? Why?"

"Say no more," Joe says as he goes back into his house and returns with a key. "Just fill her up before you bring her back, please."

Dr. Francis grabs the key and walks away without a response. You get into Joe's car with him. It's an old, rusted over Nova with no air conditioning.

"He seems like a nice guy," you say.

"Everyone's nice when they owe you a thousand dollars but they never have any money to pay you back," he says.

"I wish I had a thousand dollars," you say, imagining all the things you could buy with that much money. "What'd he need the money for?"

Dr. Francis drives the Nova out of the yard and onto the road. "You're sitting in it."

You roll your window down to let some air in as he flies down the highway. You can't stop thinking about the vials and how much the powers could help the world. "Why do you think the powers are a problem?"

"What?"

"The side effects from your formula that you talked about," you remind him. "Why are they a bad thing?"

He sighs and says, "Roll your window up." He rolls his up too so you can hear each other. "I was working with the military when I made this discovery. Ava was my assistant. I couldn't let any of them know about the side effects. I killed the project and brought all my research home. It's too dangerous for the military to have such power. They would develop super soldiers."

"That's a bad thing?" you ask in confusion.

"Not in theory. Not everyone's a good person like you though. All it would take is one bad soldier to turn the world upside down." He turns the Nova into a gas station. "Joe won't even put gas in this thing," he complains.

Your stomach growls when you smell hot dogs from the gas station store. You haven't eaten since breakfast and you're starving. "I'm gonna get some snacks," you tell Dr. Francis as he pumps gas into the car.

"We've got to get back on the road," he says. "There's no time to waste."

To stay in the car, turn to page 129.

To rush into the store, turn to page 146.

YOU OPEN YOUR DOOR as slowly and quietly as you can so Mrs. Francis doesn't try to stop you. Now close the door and run. You've only got a minute or two to get inside the store and explain everything to the security guard.

Cold air whips your face when you open the store's entrance door. You march straight to the security guard. She's wearing a black uniform with a shiny badge. She's walking between the aisles of chips and candy, searching for something to eat.

"Excuse me," you call out from behind her.

She turns in every direction. "Who said that?"

"I did," you say as you grab a chocolate bar from the shelf and hand it to her.

Her eyes get big and she puts a hand on her holster. "I don't believe in ghosts … I don't believe in ghosts," she repeats over and over.

"I'm not a ghost," you assure her. "You have to believe me. I need your help." She's frozen like a statue. "See that car at pump four?"

She turns her head to look out the glass windows and nods. "It's not here to take me to the other side, is it? I promise I can do better. I'll never lie or cheat again." Now you're not sure she can help at all.

"Just listen," you beg, exasperated. "My friends are in trouble. Mrs. Francis is trying to save her husband, but it may be too dangerous."

She nods slowly like she's in Zombieland. "Who's Mrs. Francis?"

"The lady in the car," you say.

The security guard points out the window and says, "You mean the car that's driving away?" You follow her gaze and see Mrs. Francis driving out of the gas station.

"No!" you shout as you run through the aisles and out of the store. "Mrs. Francis!" you shout after her car. "Mrs. Francis!" She doesn't hear you and keeps driving onto the busy highway.

Being invisible is cool but now you wish more than anything that people could see you. You don't know where Mrs. Francis is going or how to find her, but you suspect you'll never see her or Dr. Francis again. All you can hope for is that Kim and Kevin are okay. You wish you had stayed in the car like you were supposed to.

>>time travel back to page 51<<
THE END

KIM OPENS THE FOLDER named WORK and a video of Dr. Francis sitting at his desk begins to play. "If you're watching this video," he says, "then I'm no longer around. My dear wife and kids, please know that I love you with all of my heart. It may seem like my life revolves around my work, but nothing is more important to me than you."

Kevin clears his throat and looks at Kim. "Are you crying?"

She wipes her nose and says, "No. Are you?"

"My work has been based on researching and developing medicines for sicknesses and diseases in the military," Dr. Francis continues. "I've finally discovered something that can do the impossible and eradicate most of these. It has peculiar side effects though that present themselves as superpowers. I must find a way to eliminate these side effects before human trials begin."

He shakes his head and leans into the camera again. "If I've been taken, then this is the reason why. Don't look for me. It is far too dangerous. I love you." He reaches out and turns the camera off. At the same time, the folders named PANIC, LAB, and WORK disappear from the screen as if they never existed.

"I wish Mom was here to see this," Kim says to Kevin.

"I think she already knows everything," you mention. You couldn't figure out why she was in such a hurry to leave earlier but now you think you know. "She went to look for your dad."

"I hope not," Kevin says. "He said it was too dangerous." Kim agrees and grabs your house phone. She calls her mom but there's no answer.

"I'm scared," Kim admits, hugging her arms close like she's cold. "Our dad is gone and now our mom has disappeared."

"I can contact her," you tell your friends, realizing you can teleport to her car. "I can make sure she's okay."

Kim and Kevin don't think this is a good idea. They don't want to lose anyone else. They suggest you tell the officers outside everything you know.

To teleport to Mrs. Francis's car, turn to page 133.

To talk to the police, turn to page 150.

YOU STEP AWAY FROM THE CAR and plan to keep an eye on the vehicles. As soon as they leave, you'll run behind them and fly up into the air again. You head back to the gas station store so you can watch them closely.

Before you have time to turn around to face them again, both the sports car and van peel out of the gas station. You run as fast as you can behind them, just like you ran down Dr. Francis's driveway.

That should be far enough. You jump up into the air and prepare to fly again.

It doesn't work this time. Something's wrong.

The vehicles are getting farther away. You close your eyes and say, "Up, up, up." You reopen your eyes and see that you're still standing in the parking lot.

You freak out and remember Dr. Francis's words: "With someone your size and your height, my best guess is that it will work for half an hour."

You wish you had confronted Ava and the captain. Now you will never know what happens to your friends.

>>time travel back to page 100<<
THE END

THERE'S NO WAY YOU'RE TAKING A SHOT when you don't know what it'll do to you. Besides that, you hate shots!

You jump up and swat the syringe out of the lab guy's hand, snatch his keycard from him, dash out of the room, and swipe the keycard to lock him in. He yells and bangs his fist on the glass, but you can't hear anything. The glass is soundproof.

You look up and down the hall for any sign of Ava or the captain. They are nowhere in sight. You walk as quietly as you can further down the hall, searching for anyone else who may be trapped or can help you get out of here.

You're at the end of the hall now and take note of a fire extinguisher on the back wall. To your right is a lab much larger than the one in Dr. Francis's house. The walls are lined with shelves full of hundreds of vials with colorful liquid. They don't glow like the ones you destroyed.

Ava is inside, working on Dr. Francis's stolen computer. She's so entranced with the research she's reading that she doesn't notice you. You swipe the lab coat guy's keycard on a panel outside the room and walk inside.

Ava looks up at you, stands, and backs away from the computer with her hands up. She seems afraid of you. "We can change the world together," she says. "We can make it better."

You can't trust her anymore and don't believe a word she's saying. She's obviously working with the military to make soldiers stronger and faster and whatever else these vials can help them do. They're trying to create super soldiers. Maybe that's not a bad thing but it can't be good if other people have to get hurt to make it happen.

"I'm not going to help you," you tell her.

"That's too bad," she says, putting her hands down and walking up to you like she's not afraid of your strength anymore. She punches you in the arm and it hurts. "These powers are only in testing phases with mice. You are much bigger than a mouse."

You hold your arm in pain as you realize your new strength is disappearing. Ava nods toward the open door, where the captain is standing with a huge grin on his face.

You look at all the vials on the walls, unsure of what's inside them or even if any of them work. There's one orange vial that's glowing close to Ava. She must have figured out how to make it work. Drinking the orange liquid may be your only chance to get out of here.

To surrender to the captain, turn to page 136.

To drink from the orange vial, turn to page 154.

"WHAT DO WE DO NOW?" you ask Dr. Francis. Running away seems smart, but the captain will surely punish the doctor if he catches him.

"You should leave," he urges. "I don't know how long you'll be invisible. The vial you drank from was meant for a mouse. You are much bigger."

"I won't leave without you," you insist.

"You're stubborn," he says. "You shouldn't come to the research facility with me. I fear they will test the cure I created on children like you in illegal and dangerous ways."

"Why?" you ask.

The military will attempt to create child soldiers by erasing their memories and reprogramming them."

"This is what you do for them?" you ask, concerned.

"I tried to hide the cure from them," he says. "That's why I took it to my secret lab. It was meant to cure sicknesses and diseases but it has to be refined first. My assistant Ava found out about it. She hates me for hiding it."

The captain settles back into the van. "Got the other burger," he says, holding it up like a prize. "I did the work, so it's mine." He turns and faces the doctor. "The tape came off your mouth again? Whatever. Just don't whine back there."

The captain chomps down on his burger and drives the van back onto the highway. His phone rings again and he answers it with, "What? I told you I was getting burgers. No. You are not the boss. Bye!" He rolls down his window and throws the phone out.

You cover your ears as he sings along with an Ariana Grande song in his girly voice. He finally drives off the highway and through some trees in the middle of nowhere that follow a path to a guard shack.

"Want a burger?" the captain asks the security guard, handing him one. "The doctor isn't hungry."

A large metal gate opens and leads to a white warehouse that must be the research facility. The captain takes Dr. Francis inside and pushes him down a long marble hallway to the very end.

There's a huge lab here that looks just like Dr. Francis's

secret lab in his house. You're in awe of all the vials on the walls around you. They are different colors but don't glow like the ones you destroyed. Ava is in the lab.

"Time to work, doctor," Ava says when he's inside. "Be a good boy."

The captain grabs your shoulders. "Where did this twerp come from?" he asks. You look at your hands and realize you can see them again. So can everyone else.

"I bet the kid's here with the doctor," Ava surmises. She glances at him. "Right?" He shrugs his shoulders like he's never seen you before.

"It doesn't matter," Ava says. She steps up to you and looks over your arms and legs. "You're just the right age and size." She turns to the captain. "Prepare a room for memory clearance. This will be our first child super soldier."

>>time travel back to page 61<<
THE END

YOU GO TO THE BACK OF THE ROOM and act like you're reading the labels on the stockpile of food. There are cans of fruits and vegetables and candy bars that say MRE on them. Water bottles are all over.

You close your eyes and picture the captain's camouflaged military van. You try to picture his face but it's a blur. You vaguely remember seeing a tattoo on his arm that looked like a frog skeleton. Open your eyes again.

You're sitting in a back seat of the military van, next to Dr. Francis. His hands are tied and there's duct tape over his mouth. His eyes are big like he doesn't believe you're really here. He grunts as if he's trying to tell you something.

"Quiet down back there, doctor!" the captain yells from up front. "I don't think we need you, but lucky for you, Ava does." You crouch down as low as you can so he can't see you. He looks back twice but you're sure he doesn't see you.

The captain puts a cell phone to his ear and says, "Yeah, I need gas before we get out there. Sounds good." He drives the van into the next gas station and parks at a pump. You sit up when he steps out and see Ava's car in front of the van. You rip the duct tape off Dr. Francis's mouth before you do anything else.

"He saw you," Dr. Francis says immediately. "I was trying to say that he saw you."

The van door on your side slides open and the captain pokes his head in to say, "Hey, how you doing?" before he grabs you and pulls you out.

Ava walks up and jabs you in the arm with a needle. It burns! "Good catch," she says to the captain. "This one is perfect."

The captain ties your hands behind you and tosses you back into the van. "Teleporting? Really?" he says to Ava. "This is getting weirder and weirder." He slides the door shut. You rub your arm against the seat because it still burns.

"She neutralized your power," the doctor says. "You won't be able to teleport again or have any other power."

The captain gets back into the driver's seat and says, "Hey! No talking!" He follows Ava back onto the highway and drives for an hour. Now he's turning down a dirt road in the middle of nowhere.

The road leads to a guard shack, where a uniformed man steps out and waves the van and car through. A large metal gate opens and reveals a white warehouse behind it.

"It's a research facility," Dr. Francis whispers.

"So they can run experiments on children," you mumble, feeling sick. The van stops and the captain gets out.

"I'm sorry for what's going to happen to you," Dr. Francis says. "You don't deserve this."

The van door slides open and the captain yanks you out. He leads you to the facility and down a long marble hallway, where he throws you into a room with a cold metal bed. There's a large window facing the hallway so anyone can see in. Dr. Francis is thrown into the room across from yours.

Ava steps into your room and says, "Thank you for

volunteering." A man in a lab coat joins her. He's got a syringe in his hand and is squirting liquid up into the air from it.

"I've already had the shot," you remind Ava.

She chuckles. "That was just to keep you from teleporting. Can't have you running off and reporting us." She grabs the needle from the man in the lab coat. "This one is to make sure you can never leave this room."

The captain walks in and holds you still while Ava approaches you with the needle. You swallow hard and wonder if things would have been different if you had teleported to Ava's car instead of the captain's van.

>>time travel back to page 64<<
THE END

YOU STEP OFF THE BUS and blast into the sky as the passengers cheer in awe. It's easier to control your flying now, but something feels different. It feels like your body is heavier and you won't be able to fly as long as before.

You head over the same houses and cars you passed on the way here. You can't stay as high as you did the first time but you're still making good time. There's no way you can track Ava down now so you head back to Dr. Francis's house. You've got to get him untied and come up with a plan to find your friends.

You land in his driveway but not as smoothly as you landed on the dirt road. Your legs are wobbly and you stumble. The doctor rushes out of his house to greet you.

"Thank goodness you're safe," he says. "What happened to the bomb?"

You tell him that you got rid of it and no one was hurt. He's grateful to you. "How did you get untied?" you ask.

"I may be old," he says, "but I was a Boy Scout when I was your age. I know how to tie and untie all kinds of knots. It just takes me longer now."

"What about Kim, Kevin, and Mrs. Francis?" you ask him. "How are we going to find them?" He shakes his head and leads you back into the house.

"It's been an hour since they may have been sealed inside the panic room," he explains. "The room is soundproof. I really don't know if they're in there. We'll find out for sure in another hour when the seal breaks."

"Panic room?" you ask as he leads you into the kitchen and to the food pantry. He rotates the shelves to the side and reveals a hidden steel door.

"When I put in the computer code to seal you in my secret lab, I also put in a code that warned my family to hide in the panic room," he says. He points to a light bulb in the kitchen. "It flashes red when I warn them to hide inside. There is one in every room of this house."

"Are they inside?" you wonder out loud.

Dr. Francis shrugs and walks out of the kitchen. "The room door opens automatically within two hours unless they delay it. My family can see us out here but we can't see them." He sighs and sits on a couch in the living room. "Ava and her henchman stole my computer with all my research. I also stored live video and remote access codes for the panic room on there."

You wonder if it was smart to do that. Hackers love to steal information from computers.

"Don't worry," Dr. Francis advises, seeing the concern on your face. "That computer is not on any networks and has no access to the internet."

"How did Ava know about the vials?" you ask.

He runs his hands through his hair. "She was my lab assistant earlier this year, but I had to fire her. During my medical research, I discovered a way to cure many disabilities in mice."

You remember watching Kim's slow mouse race around the

mouse wheel earlier today. "And if it works in mice, then it works in humans?" you ask.

"Usually, yes," he says. "But it takes years of testing to rule out all potential harmful side effects. We found that the most common side effects the mice developed were extraordinary powers."

"Like flying," you whisper.

"The vial you drank from was meant for a mouse. You are much larger than that. That means your ability to fly won't last anywhere near as long as a mouse's."

You think about how your body felt heavier when you flew back here and how you couldn't fly as high as before. Is the power wearing off?

You jump when you hear sirens nearby.

"I called the police," the doctor says. "I didn't want to because I'm not sure who I can trust. But my family may be in danger and I have to do everything in my power to protect them."

You realize that your friends are probably safe in the panic room but no one knows for sure yet. Ava could have taken them. You keep hearing her voice in your head when she told the captain, "I have experiments to run on the children."

Dr. Francis steps outside to meet the police officers. You wonder if they have any way to find your friends if Ava has taken them or whether it's impossible with the military involved. You have a better chance of finding them yourself from high in the sky.

To stay and give information to the police, turn to page 144.

To fly off and search for Ava's car, turn to page 160.

YOU WAIT FOR DR. FRANCIS to finish filling up the gas tank and get back onto the road. "We'll be there soon," he says.

"Where?" you ask, realizing he never told you.

"Why? What do they have to do with anything?"

He takes a deep breath. "Ava's trying to punish me. I withheld my research from her. She figured it out after I left but didn't have all the pieces."

"That's why she stole your research," you say.

He nods. "I believe my formulas work best on children and teenagers. She'll try it on my kids and compare the results with my wife. If she can prove it works best on kids, the military will put that to use."

"You're talking about kid soldiers," you say in amazement and fear. "That can't be legal." You wonder how powerful you truly are and if you'd ever be a soldier at your age.

"Child super soldiers," he reminds you as he turns the Nova down a hidden dirt road and parks on the side. "There's a guard shack up ahead. They're not going to let us in." He pats your shoulder. "This is your last chance to get out. I'm going to drive through the gate."

To get out of the car, turn to page 164.

To stay in the car, turn to page 184.

YOU WATCH AS MRS. FRANCIS ARGUES with the guard. He won't back down and neither will she. He finally steps back into the shack behind him and picks up a phone. "Yeah," he says into it. "Okay."

The gate in front of you opens enough for two soldiers to step through from the other side and closes again. One stands in front of the car and the other approaches Mrs. Francis's window.

"Ma'am, I suggest you leave or you'll be arrested for interfering with military operations," he says.

"I'm not going anywhere without my husband," she insists.

"Step out of the vehicle," the soldier orders.

"Open the gate," she responds.

"Step out of the vehicle now," he says again. "You and the kid."

Mrs. Francis jerks her head toward you as the soldier opens her door and pulls her out. You hold your hands in front of your face and realize you can see them again. Your door opens and the second soldier orders you out.

"Yeah," you hear the security guard say into his phone. "The doctor's wife and a kid. Okay." He sets the phone down and calls out to the soldiers, "She wants them both for research."

The gate opens and you're taken to a large white warehouse that must be the research facility. You and Mrs. Francis are led down a long marble hallway and tossed into different rooms.

Ava appears in your room with an old man in a lab coat.

132

He gives you a shot and lays you down on a cold metal bed.

"This is perfect," Ava says. "You're just the right age and size. You will be the first child soldier with superpowers to help us take over the world." She smiles and pats you on the head. "Thank you for volunteering."

>time travel back to page 97<<

>>time travel back to page 97<<
THE END

YOU CLOSE YOUR EYES and picture Mrs. Francis's car. It's white and has five seats that are brown, an air freshener hanging from the rearview mirror, and a picture of Kim and Kevin on the driver's sun visor. Now open your eyes.

You're sitting in the front passenger seat of Mrs. Francis's car but she isn't here. There's a gas station in front of you that you can see through the windshield. You get out of the car and go inside the store.

You're looking around but Mrs. Francis isn't in sight. A lady security guard is in the frozen food section, looking at tacos.

"Excuse me," you say as you approach her. She turns to you and smiles.

"What can I do for you?" she asks, returning her attention to the tacos.

"I'm looking for my friends' mom," you tell her. "She's about your age but a little taller. She wears glasses and has short brown hair."

"Yeah," the security guard says toward the freezer. "I think I saw her in the back, by the restrooms." She absently waves a finger in that direction. You thank her and head that way.

"I wouldn't eat those tacos," a store clerk says as he passes you and stands by the security guard. "They'll mess up your stomach."

Mrs. Francis is walking out the front door. You call out her name and join her. "How did you ... oh, right," she says. "Where are Kim and Kevin? Are they okay?"

You assure her that they're fine and tell her about the video the three of you watched on your computer. "You know where he is, don't you?" you ask her, referring to Dr. Francis.

She sighs and nods. "He pointed to a hidden path once when we passed it. There's a secret research facility at the end of it. I think they took him there. And I think I can find it again."

"You can't do that," you urge her. "Dr. Francis said it's too dangerous."

"Go back home," she insists. She walks to her car and opens the door. "You're a good kid, but I'm going to do whatever it takes to keep my family together."

"Wait," you say before she gets into the car. "You can't do this on your own. I'm the only one who can get close to Ava and the captain without them knowing. I just have to see the place where Dr. Francis is." You realize you can teleport in and out as long as you can picture the settings.

"That's a horrible idea," she says as she gets into the car and closes the door. She puts the car in reverse but stops and rolls her window down. "If we do this, we do it together."

To go with Mrs. Francis,
turn to page 168.

To go back home,
turn to page 188.

YOU TAKE A DEEP BREATH, let go of the van's roof, and roll off into a dumpster full of trash bags. Your feet slam against the dumpster's green metal wall and the back of your head lands on top of a bag of what smells like steak and French fries.

You sit up, feeling exhausted and weak, and watch the van drive off. You can't stay here. You've got to keep up with the van and sports car.

You jump out of the dumpster and run so you can take off into the sky again. But you have to stop. Your head is spinning and the road is blurry. Everything around you is blurry.

You vaguely see the van getting farther and farther away, like a square becoming smaller and smaller. Now the square is gone.

You're not willing to accept this. You've got to save your friends if they're in Ava's car. You close your eyes and say, "Up, up, up," trying to force your body into the sky.

Yes! You feel your body rising.

You reopen your eyes and crash to the pavement. Your body couldn't go high that time. Maybe you can't fly right now because your body feels busted up. Maybe you'll never fly again. Dr. Francis was afraid this would happen.

You should have tried to hold on to the van longer. Now you may never see your friends again.

>>time travel back to page 54<<
THE END

YOU DON'T KNOW IF THE OTHER VIALS have been tested and if they can hurt you. You stand in place while the captain grabs your arm and leads you out of the lab. Why did he have to grab the same arm Ava punched you in? It hurts!

As you're taken back down the hall, you see that each of the other rooms has a person in it now. They all look like teenagers. You wonder if they have powers like you did and if they're here to be experimented on like mice.

The teenagers bang with all their might on the glass as if they think you can get them out. There's no sound, but the vibrations make your body tense the same way it does when you hear fingernails drag down a chalkboard.

"Cut it out!" the captain shouts. He lets go of your arm and spins around in a circle so all of the rooms can hear him. Maybe he's never been shut in one of the rooms and doesn't realize they can't hear him. "Stop banging on the glass!"

You wish you could help the teenagers get out of here but this is probably your last chance to run. You take off while the captain is facing the other direction and shouting nonsense.

You can make it out of here. The front door isn't far away. You just have to be fast. You can do it.

The man in the lab coat steps out of the room you locked him in and jabs you in the arm with the syringe you avoided. The captain must have set him free.

Your legs are weak and you crash toward the floor. The captain catches you and carries you back to your room, where he tosses you on the cold metal bed. You don't feel it though.

You don't feel anything. You can't move.

"Nice try," the captain says. "Looks like you're not going anywhere. I win."

>>time travel back to page 118<<
THE END

DR. FRANCIS STANDS as John and the captain come into the office. "What's the meaning of this?" he asks.

The captain steps up and grabs Dr. Francis's arm. "Let's go."

"Leave him alone!" you shout.

"Who said that?" the captain asks, searching the room with his eyes.

"There's no one else here," John says. "This is getting too weird. Please take the doctor and go."

The captain forces Dr. Francis out of the office and back into the van. He ties the doctor's wrists and legs back up. You join him again as the van continues to the research facility.

You end up at a large white warehouse hidden in the middle of the woods. There's a party bus outside that seems out of place. The doctor is taken inside the facility and led down a long marble hallway with rooms on both sides of it. There's a teenager in each room you pass.

The doctor is thrown into a room with a metal bed. What exactly is going on here? Is Ava around, experimenting on these teenagers? You can go into the room with Dr. Francis before it's locked or you can stay in the hall and try to figure a way out of here.

To go into the room with Dr. Francis, turn to page 178.

To stay in the hall and find a way out, turn to page 194.

YOU CLOSE YOUR EYES AND IMAGINE being in the store with aisles of potato chips, candy, and drinks. Open your eyes.

You're standing in an aisle with potato chip bags on both sides. At the end of the aisle is a store clerk setting up a ladder beneath a light that's out way up high on the ceiling.

There's the security guard by the cash register, talking to the cashier. You walk briskly to her. "I'm thinking about tacos for lunch," she says to the cashier. She's wearing a neatly pressed uniform and has a nightstick attached to her belt.

"Excuse me," you say from behind her.

The security guard turns and says, "Hi. Can I help you?" Her nametag says Shannon. You're not sure she can help but maybe she has training for situations like the one Dr. Francis is in.

"My friend's been kidnapped," you blurt. You wonder how much to tell her.

"What?" she says, giving you her full attention. "When?"

"His name is Dr. Francis and he's in the back of that military van," you say faster than a tornado spins and point at the captain's ride.

Ava is staring at you when you point toward her and she says something to the captain. He quickly gets back into the van while she jumps into her sports car and peels out of the gas station.

"Call the cops," the guard tells the cashier before she rushes out the front door.

The cashier dials 911 and covers the phone speaker with her hand. "She thinks she's a cop but she's not," she says to you. "She's failed the test like a million times."

The guard's car screeches as it zooms out of the parking lot and onto the highway. "She's not…" you start to say.

"Oh, yeah," the cashier replies, shaking her head. "She's crazy. She's going after them." The cashier takes her hand off the phone speaker and says, "Yes, I need to report a kidnapping."

You've got to stop the guard. She has no idea how dangerous Ava and the captain are. You close your eyes and imagine being in the guard's car. It looks like a police car—sirens and everything. The guard has braided hair and brown eyes. Open your eyes.

You're sitting in the front passenger seat of the guard's car. She shrieks and nearly drives off the road when sees you.

"What are you … how are you …" she says in short breaths.

"I'm only here to warn you and help my friend," you assure her.

"I don't believe in ghosts," she claims, staring straight ahead and squeezing her eyes open and close. "I don't believe in ghosts … I don't … I don't … I don't believe in ghosts."

"I'm not a ghost," you tell her, hardly believing she thinks you are. "I'm just a kid. I teleported here." She gives you a sideways glance so you explain everything that happened back at Dr. Francis's house.

"You're a good kid," Shannon says, warming up to you.

"Even if you're not a ghost." You both laugh. "I probably shouldn't be following Ava and the captain but I have to."

"Why?"

She takes a deep breath and squints at you like she's deciding if she should tell you her reasons. "Everyone in my family is a police officer. My mom. My dad. My sister." She shrugs. "Everyone but me."

The van and sports car slow and turn down a hidden dirt road covered by trees. Shannon keeps her car far back so they aren't suspicious. "One ... two ... three..."

"What are you doing?" you interrupt.

"Hide-and-seek rules," she explains.

"What?"

"Eight ... nine ... ten," she says and stops counting. "Ready or not, here I come." She turns down the same hidden dirt road and drives for a mile before reaching a guard shack.

"How's it going?" she says to the man in the shack after rolling her window down. He's wearing on the same uniform as the captain and has a clipboard in his hands. "I need to get inside," she says, pointing to the tall metal gate in front of you. She flashes her security badge.

"Sorry, ma'am," the man tells her like he's not sorry at all. "These grounds are for military personnel only. You need to turn around and get back on the highway." He stops and does a double take at her face. "Shannon, is that you?"

She throws her head back as if she's surprised he knows her name. "Wait ... Phil?" He smiles and nods. Shannon hits the back of her hand against your shoulder. "This is Phil," she says to you. "We went to security school together."

"Longest forty hours of my life," Phil adds. "Didn't recognize you at first."

Shannon pats her stomach and laughs. "I've been eating a few tacos." She gets out of the car and hugs Phil before leading him away while they discuss memories of the class. Her hand is behind her back and she's waving it at you like she wants you to do something.

You realize she wants you to teleport inside the guard shack while Phil is distracted. From there you can open the gate. You close your eyes and envision everything you saw through the shack's windows. Open your eyes.

You're still in the car. You remember that Mrs. Francis said your ability wouldn't last forever. You close your eyes and try again. Same thing.

Your only option is to get out of the car and walk into the shack, hoping Phil doesn't see or hear you. You could be in big trouble if you get caught. No, that's not the only option. You can sit right here and wait for Shannon to come back. Maybe she has another idea.

To wait for Shannon to come back,
turn to page 180.

To go into the guard shack,
turn to page 197.

YOU MEET TWO OFFICERS at the front door with Dr. Francis. One of the officers is a short lady and the other is man built like a mountain. They nod at you as they enter the house.

"Sorry it took us so long to get here," the lady officer says. "There's a mess out on Ford Road and the whole force is working on it."

The male officer adds, "Someone tried to blow up a bus with dozens of passengers on it."

"They're all okay, right?" you ask right away. Everyone on the bus was shaken but it doesn't seem like any of them were hurt. You would never have left if you had thought someone needed help.

"Yeah," the lady officer confirms. "They say some kid helped them then flew off." She clears her throat. "They think it was an angel."

"My family was attacked," Dr. Francis interrupts.

"Right, sorry," the tall officer says. "Do you have any pictures of them?" Dr. Francis grabs a family picture off a coffee table and hands it to him.

"Tell us exactly what happened," the short officer says, writing in a notebook.

Dr. Francis relays how Ava and the captain came into the home and tied him up. That they may have taken the family to experiment on them. Then they left a bomb to destroy him and his research.

The officers glance at each other and shake their heads like this is the craziest story they've ever heard. The short officer stops writing and puts her notebook away. "Where is this bomb now?"

Dr. Francis rubs his temple. "It's gone," he finally says. "Look, forget I said that. I just need to know that my family is safe. They could be in the panic room or my assistant could be experimenting on them."

"You need to come downtown with us," the tall officer says. "We'll get you the help you need." He's looking at Dr. Francis like he's a dangerous criminal mastermind.

"It's my fault," you say. You tell them how you drank from the vial and flew away to take the bomb to a safe location and it almost demolished the bus.

You and the doctor are arrested and committed to a psychiatric hospital for the criminally insane.

>>time travel back to page 128<<
THE END

YOU GET OUT OF THE CAR, run into the store, and head straight for the candy aisle. You're starving—maybe it's because your new power is burning a ton of calories.

"Help!" you hear a woman shout from the front of the store.

You look down the aisle to see a cashier holding a piece of paper and a young guy with a crew cut standing in front of her. He's holding a fist in front of her.

A female security guard approaches him. "Nobody has to get hurt. If it's money you want, you can have it." She nods at the cashier. "Right, Mary?"

Mary already has her register open and is pulling money out of it as fast as he can. "Right."

You don't know what's on the paper Mary has but imagine it's a robbery note threatening harm. You sense the cashier and security guard are in more danger than they realize. Maybe there's something you can do to help. You're invincible and strong enough to take down a man as large as the captain.

You take a deep break, grab a candy bar, and walk up to the cashier's counter. The robber is on your left and the security guard is on your right. Her eyes are big, like she can't believe you're crazy enough to stand there.

"Hey!" the robber shouts at you. "What do you think you're doing?" He glances from person to person as if he's confused. "Can't you see I'm robbing this joint?"

You put the candy bar on the counter and turn to him. "You should walk away. I don't want to hurt you."

He stares at you for a moment and laughs. "You? Hurt me?"

He looks over you at the cashier as if you're invisible. "Hurry up with my money!"

You push your hands against his chest while he's ignoring you. His body slides across the floor and slams into an aisle of potato chips. Bags full of every flavor of chips fall on top of and all around him.

The security guard rushes to him and checks his pockets. He never had a weapon. He only pretended to so he could get the money. "Call the police!" she shouts to Mary. She looks at you in amazement. "What are they feeding you kids these days?"

You put five dollars on the counter and tell the cashier to keep the change. You grab your purchase and hold it up for the security guard to see. "Candy bars," you say as you nod at her and walk out of the store.

Turn to page 129

YOU QUIETLY OPEN YOUR DOOR and slip out while the guard is distracted with Mrs. Francis. You make it to the guard shack and locate a remote keypad that has a button with the words Open Gate. You press the button and put the keypad in your pocket as the gate begins to open.

The guard rushes back into the shack and searches for the remote. You walk around him and swipe the security card from his belt and head back to the car.

"We make a good team," Mrs. Francis says when you open the car door and get back in. "Let's find my husband and get out of here." Two soldiers appear from behind the gate and block the car before you can go anywhere. Mrs. Francis reaches across your seat and throws your door open. "It's up to you," she whispers.

You're the only one who can get past the gate now. You step back out of the car and walk past the soldiers. Now that you're past the open gate you can see a large white warehouse. You open the front door and go inside.

A long marble hallway is in front of you. There are dozens of rooms on each side of it with huge windows. You walk down the hall and observe there's a metal bed in each room but the rooms are otherwise empty. You look for Dr. Francis in every room.

There he is! You see him standing with his back to the window. You try to open the door, but the knob won't budge. There's some kind of security panel on the door that needs a keycard. You wonder if the security card you took from the guard will work here. You swipe it over the panel and the door unlocks.

You go to the doctor and find that he's weak and can barely stand. "What did they do to you?" you ask, not expecting an answer.

"You," he says as you help him to the door. "You're Kim and Kevin's friend." You're surprised he can see you. You look at your hands and realize you can see them again.

"Going somewhere?" a deep voice calls out as you exit the room. It's the captain and he does not look happy.

"The end of the hall," Dr. Francis whispers to you. "A lab like mine. Drink the white vial. Be a cheetah." You know that cheetahs are superfast. He's telling you to run as fast as you can to a lab in here.

To run to the lab,
turn to page 166.

To stay with the doctor,
turn to page 187.

KIM MARCHES OUTSIDE and tells the police about the video you just watched. The same two officers you talked to earlier come into the house.

"Let me get this straight," the lady officer says. "There were videos about your father and clues about his disappearance but they erased themselves?"

"Yes," Kevin says, standing with his sister. "That's exactly what happened."

"I remember you," the man officer says, pointing to you. "Aren't you the kid that can teleport?" The lady officer chuckles.

"That's right," Kim assures him. "Show them," she says to you. You're not sure it's a good idea, but the officers don't look like they believe any of what's being said. There's only one way to prove it to them and then they'll listen.

"Okay," you say, "everyone stand back." You close your eyes and focus on your front yard so they can clearly see you disappear and then reappear out there. Now open your eyes.

The officers are staring at you with raised eyebrows. Nothing happened. You're standing in the same place you were before you closed your eyes.

"Go ahead," Kevin says. "Show them." You nod and loosen your shoulders then jump up and down.

"Okay, here we go," you tell them. You close your eyes again and focus on the yard. You can feel it. It's working this time. Open your eyes.

The officers are shaking their heads at you. "We have serious matters to take of," the man officer scolds. "No more games." He looks around the house. "And where is the lady watching you?"

"Our mom is in the bathroom," Kevin lies. The officers nod at each other and leave to go back across the street.

"What happened?" Kim asks you.

"I don't know," you admit, frustrated. "It doesn't work anymore." You sit with her and Kevin by the phone, hoping to hear good news from Mrs. Francis, but you never hear from her again. You wish you had teleported to her car when you could have.

>>time travel back to page 99<<
THE END

YOU WAVE YOUR HANDS in front of you to stop the young man as he passes you.

"Yeah?" he says, holding the phone away from his ear.

"I need your phone," you tell him.

He huffs at you and puts the phone back to his ear. "Can you believe this kid is trying to get my phone?" He brushes past you, laughing as he opens the store door and goes inside. Cool air whips past you and the smell of hot dogs fills the air before the door closes.

You notice for the first time that a security guard's car is in the parking lot. The security guard is at a cash register, buying tacos. She's wearing a black uniform with a shiny badge.

Ava and the captain are still out of sight. You pull the glass doors open and rush into the store. You run to the guard at the cash register and say, "Help. My friends are in trouble."

"That kid tried to steal my cell phone," the young man you saw outside says. "Don't believe anything the kid says." The phone is still plastered to his ear. "Yes, I made sure it's fat free," he says into the phone.

The guard looks from you to the young man and sighs. She slides her credit card at the cash register and takes her tacos. "I shouldn't eat these," she says. "They always mess up my stomach."

"My friends have been taken by a man and woman outside," you tell the guard. "I needed a phone to call the police."

She stares at you for a moment and sets her tacos back on

the counter. "Show me." She turns to the cashier and says, "Call the police."

You lead her to the front door and out into the parking lot. Now your friends will be safe.

The military van and sports car are gone.

"We've got to find them!" you shout. You run through the parking lot and try to fly off into the sky like before, but when you jump, you land on your feet. "Fly!" you shout. "Up, up, up!"

The young man with the cell phone steps out and shrugs at the guard. "I told you not to believe the kid."

You stop and take in deep breaths. Dr. Francis warned you that you may not be able to fly for more than 30 minutes.

You should have tried to get your friends out of the car. Now you will never know what happens to them.

>>time travel back to page 81<<
THE END

YOU SNATCH THE VIAL with orange liquid off the shelf, flick the cap off, and swallow the contents as fast as you can. You close your eyes when the captain lunges at you.

Nothing happens so you reopen your eyes, confused. You're standing outside of the room, watching the captain peel himself off the floor. How did you get here?

The captain and Ava stare at you, looking as bewildered as you feel. That only lasts for a second, though, because now he's charging at the door, straight for you.

You quickly swipe the lab coat man's keycard over the panel in front of the door again and it closes just before the captain reaches it, locking him and Ava in. You rip the fire extinguisher off the back wall and pound it against the security panel until it sparks and breaks apart.

You watch through the glass as the captain throws his arms up at Ava and they argue. You don't know how you did it but you teleported. It seems like you're able to move from one location to another just by closing your eyes and wishing for it. This is amazing.

You sense vibrations from the glass all throughout the hall. You walk away from outside the lab and carefully investigate.

To your surprise, each room has a teenager in it now. The captain must have brought them here, but where did they come from? They need as much help as you do. You close your eyes and focus on teleporting into the nearest room to get some answers before letting them out.

You reopen your eyes as a teenager jumps back from you,

surprised you appeared from thin air. He's wearing a bathing suit, tank top, and sandals.

"What's your name?" you ask him.

"Miguel," he says quietly. You tell him your name and how you got here. He's not afraid of you anymore.

"Me and my friends were on a bus trip to a water park," Miguel explains. "The bus never made it there. It brought us here." He shakes his head and runs a hand through his hair. "When we got here, three men in military uniforms locked us in these rooms."

The captain must have been one of those men, meaning there are two more soldiers here somewhere. Miguel says he saw them come from a small cabin next to this building when the bus arrived.

He pulls a cell phone out of his pocket and holds it up. "I was going to call 911 but I can't get a signal in here." You realize that the signals have been blocked from here somehow. The phone may work if you can get outside.

"Can I see that?" you ask him.

"Sure." He hands it to you, and you see there is less than one bar in signal strength. You can't make or receive any calls or texts. but maybe you can get the GPS coordinates of where you are.

The coordinates appear after several attempts and you text them to 911 with a message that kid hostages are being held here. Texting 911 doesn't work everywhere but it does work in many locations when there's an emergency you can't call for.

The text won't go out from here but it's ready when you get outside.

You take the keycard out of your pocket, hand it to Miguel, and tell him to let his friends out. You've got to teleport out of this building so the 911 text can be sent without drawing attention to any of your captors.

You've learned that the power you have won't last forever because it was meant for a mouse. You may only be able to use it one more time. You can teleport outside the warehouse, verify the text goes through, then make sure the teenagers get out of here safely. Or you can teleport back to Dr. Francis's house to make sure he and his family are okay and the text will still go through.

To teleport back to Dr. Francis's house, turn to page 175.

To teleport outside the research center, turn to page 192.

YOU NOTICE THERE'S A DOOR in the back of the room and quickly lock the office door. Dr. Francis opens the back door and walks through it to find a hallway inside that leads to a restroom. You search with him for any way out and conclude there's nothing here but a sink and toilet.

The captain barges in and grabs Dr. Francis. To your surprise, he also grabs you! You look at your hands and can see them again.

"Who are you?" the captain asks in a threatening voice.

"I've never seen this kid before," Dr. Francis lies.

The captain looks to John but he just shrugs. "Must have come off the streets," John finally says. "Get out of here," he says to you. "And don't come back." He escorts you outside the building.

The captain shoves Dr. Francis back into the van and drives off. You didn't get the license number. You have no idea where the research facility is. All you can do is tell your story to the police.

Dr. Francis is never found again. His whole family disappears and their lives are reenacted one day on a TV special about families that vanished without a trace.

>>time travel back to page 104<<
THE END

IT'S TOO RISKY TO LEAVE the car right now because Ava could be done pumping gas any minute and get back into the car. It's taking longer than you thought, but she's getting into her seat now. She drives out of the station and back onto the highway.

Ava turns the radio up loud, the same way you turn up the music in your room. She puts her cellphone to her ear and talks but you can't hear what she says.

She finally turns down a dirt road and stops after a mile. She rolls down her window and says, "Yeah, in the back."

The back door by you opens and a man in the same uniform as the captain says to you, "Get out." You realize Ava saw you at the gas station and reported it to this guard.

You close your eyes and imagine being back with Mrs. Francis, Kim, and Kevin. When you reopen your eyes, you're still in the car. Mrs. Francis was right when she said your ability to teleport wouldn't work forever. You get out of the car slowly.

"Put your hands behind your back," the guard orders. He ties your hands and put you back into the car.

"Thank you," Ava says in a high pitch and drives through an open metal gate. She adjusts her rearview mirror so she can see you behind her. "You teleported here, didn't you? You drank one of the vials." You turn your head and don't answer. "It works," she says excitedly.

The car stops in front of a white warehouse. Ava opens her door and steps out to meet the captain. He has Dr. Francis by his side as a prisoner. "The project can move forward," Ava tells the captain. "We will have child super soldiers."

She opens your door and tells you to get out. "Don't worry, kid. You won't remember any of this after I erase your memory. Thank you for being the first volunteer."

>>time travel back to page 106<<
THE END

YOU RUSH THROUGH THE HOUSE and out the back door. You're the only one who can find the yellow sports car in time and that's what you're going to do. You jump up into the air and take off.

Your feet drag against tall plants and hedges as you try to go higher. Your arms and legs feel like they weigh a ton. You've got to fight through it and fly higher. Your friends need you. You take a deep breath and focus on the power lines above you because you've got to get at least that high so you don't crash into anything.

That's it ... higher ... higher ... you're doing it ... there you go!

Now follow the road in the same direction you watched the sports car and camouflaged van speed off in earlier. That was at least ten minutes ago and they could be far away now, but you're not willing to give up.

From up here you can see all the cars and all the buildings the car and van could be parked at. They're not at the gas station. They're not at any of the stop lights.

Keep going.

You're coming up on the part of town that's mostly covered in trees. There aren't many places out here for a car to park. Maybe it's time to give up. The sun is starting to go down. Your body feels so heavy that you know you won't be able to fly much longer. You hate to admit it but it's time to turn around and get back to familiar territory.

But ... wait. What is that yellow speck deep in the woods?

Could that be…?

Fly closer.

It's the yellow sports car!

You fly down and land clumsily on a hidden car path in the woods. You suspect you won't be able to fly again and hope you can make it out of here. Ava's car and the captain's van are parked in front of you, facing the front of a large white warehouse. There's a security check-in booth behind you. Is this some type of military installation?

You quickly and quietly walk up to the sports car and camouflaged van. The car windows are tinted dark but the car appears to be empty. The van is also empty. You look straight ahead at the warehouse just as the front door bursts open and the captain rushes out. You duck behind the car and watch him run down a path to a smaller building.

You stand back up, hurry to the warehouse entrance, take a deep breath and pull the door open. You're shocked at what you see inside.

A marble hall runs down the middle of the warehouse. On each side are maybe a dozen rooms with large glass windows. You walk down the hall and see there is a teenager in each room. There is also a medical bed and equipment to monitor them.

You walk faster and search for Kim and Kevin. Their mom could be here too. You're not sure how much time you have before the captain comes back so you shout their names as you pass each room.

"Kim!"

"Kevin!"

"Mrs. Francis!"

Someone bangs on the window of the room ahead of you on the right side. You run as fast as you can to it. This is it. You're going to get them out.

You stop in front of the window, shocked. Your friends aren't inside. The person you're looking at is the teenager you talked to on the bus you stopped. His name is Miguel.

He's shouting something at you, but you can't hear him through the glass. It's so thick that you can only sense vibrations. You feel devastated because you helped protect him once before but you're not sure if you can now.

There's got to be a way to get into the rooms. You look to the next room after his, the last one on the right side. You see another familiar face—Ava's.

The room she's in looks eerily similar to Dr. Francis's secret lab, but this one has shelves full of vials with colored liquid that don't glow. Ava is working on the computer she stole from Dr. Francis. She doesn't see you but seems to be rushing as she mixes two vials of green and red liquid together.

The front door of the warehouse opens and sunlight pours in. The room across from the lab has a wide-open door. You duck inside.

Many footsteps race down the hall toward the room you're in. They must have seen you. This is the end.

The footsteps stop in the hall in front of the room you're

hiding in. You hear a beeping sound from the room across from you and then the footsteps disappear into it.

The next voice you hear belongs to Ava. "You're making a mistake. Don't do this. Just let them go." Her voice trails off as the footsteps get farther and farther away until the front door opens and closes again.

You stand and look down the hall to verify no one is there. It's empty. Now the lab door is open. You don't know when the warehouse's front door will open again or even if you can get out of here without getting caught.

You consider drinking another vial because it may somehow give you the power to get the teenagers out of here. On the other hand, the captain and the people with him just left and now's probably the best time to make a run for it, leaving the teenagers behind. Your friends aren't here so they're probably in the panic room in their home.

To go into the lab and drink from a vial, turn to page 181.

To run out of here as fast as you can, turn to page 200.

YOU GET OUT OF THE CAR and close your door. "Please don't do this," you say to Dr. Francis through your open window. "There has to be another way."

He avoids your eyes and drives back onto the dirt road, accelerating to full speed. The car seems to get smaller and smaller as gets farther away until he disappears.

You hear the bang of metal against metal as he crashes through the gate ahead. He could be hurt. You run as fast as you can down the dirt run toward him.

You're almost out of breath but you see the guard shack and the broken gate behind it. The Nova is parked further back, in front of a large white warehouse that must be the research facility.

"Hey!" a guard shouts at you from outside the shack. He's on a phone, no doubt warning Ava and whoever else is inside the facility. "Stop right there!"

You freeze, unsure of what to do, but jump when a large bus directly behind you honks its obnoxiously loud horn, giving you a heart attack. The guard reaches you and tells you to come with him.

You've got to do whatever you can to protect yourself. If the guard takes you into that facility, you may never get out. You push your hands against his chest so he flies back like the captain did. But nothing happens this time. You fear the doctor was right when he said your power may only last thirty minutes.

The guard grabs your arm and leads you to the facility.

Once inside, you're taken down a long marble hallway and locked in a room with a metal bed. A large window faces the hallway and you can see everything nearby outside. There are rooms on both sides of the hall. Is this where your friends are, trapped like you?

A line of teenagers is marched down the hall and thrown into rooms one by one. You imagine they were on the bus and have been sent here to be experimented on.

Ava enters your room with the captain. "You decided to come after all," she says, delighted. "I'm happy to see you."

"Where's Dr. Francis?" you ask her. "And where are my friends?"

"I don't know about your friends," she admits, "but the doctor is doing exactly what he's supposed to do. He may not want to, but sometimes we all have to do things we don't want to." She snaps her fingers and the captain approaches you. "Now you're going to do exactly what you're supposed to do, whether you want to or not."

The captain holds your shoulders so you can't move. An old man in a lab coat appears from behind Ava with a syringe and squirts liquid from it up into the air.

"This is where you'll spend the rest of your life," Ava says as she walks away. She turns to face you from the doorway. "Thank you for your participation."

>>time travel back to page 130<<
THE END

YOU RUN AS FAST AS YOU CAN and make it to the last rooms in the hall while the captain handles Dr. Francis. There's a large lab on the right side that looks exactly like Dr. Francis's secret lab. The walls are lined with vials full of colorful liquids that don't glow like the one you drank from. Ava is inside, mixing formulas.

You swipe the guard's security card over the key panel and the door opens. Ava stares at you with cold eyes as you enter.

"Who are you?" she asks.

You ignore her and scan the walls until you see the white vial. It's the only one that's glossy and glowing. The captain appears on the other side of the room window as he barrels down the hall to get to you. You run to the white vial and grab it as the captain barges in. You flick the cap off the vial and drink the contents before he can stop you.

Your entire body feels like it's on fire and all of your muscles scream as they stretch further than they were ever meant to. The captain stops before he reaches you and motions for Ava to stay back. They seem scared of you.

You hear a wild animal roar and realize the sound is coming from you. *Cheetah*, you think. It's the last animal Dr. Francis wanted you to think of. The white vial made your body morph into a cheetah.

"Nice kitty," the captain says timidly. You roar again, as loud as you can this time, and pounce on him, knocking him flat on his back before racing to the door. You've got to get Dr. Francis out of here before things get any weirder.

"Stop!" Ava yells. "You are the world's greatest accomplishment. Don't leave." You ignore her and zip down the hall to the doctor. He's sitting on the hallway floor.

"Get on," you tell him in a deep voice you don't recognize. It takes him a minute, but he hops on your back without any hesitation.

You make it out of the research facility and back to the open gate. You bare your magnificent fangs at the guard and soldiers around Mrs. Francis's car.

The guard locks himself in the shack and hides. The soldiers run into the woods screaming. Mrs. Francis grabs her husband, hugs him tight, and leads him to the car.

"It's you, isn't it?" she says to you.

"Yes," you answer, purring softly as she pats your head.

"You saved him," she says proudly. "Now we can tell the world what's going on here and shut this place down forever." She motions to the car. "Get in the back. Don't scratch up my seats."

You all head back to their house and arrive just as the safe room unlocks. Kim and Kevin step out unharmed.

You saved the day. You are a true superhero!

THE END

"WHAT ELSE DO YOU KNOW?" Mrs. Francis asks as she drives onto the highway. Her words remind you of the doctor when you walked into his office and he said, "How much did you see?"

"I know my ability to teleport is a side effect of the medication," you respond. "It may not last forever."

She purses her lips and nods like she's impressed. "My husband has been working his whole life to make the world better for everyone. The medicine will work for 99% of the population, but it's twice as effective on young people."

"You're talking about kids," you whisper, realizing why Ava wants to experiment on children.

"Ava found my husband's research," Mrs. Francis says, adjusting the rearview mirror, "and is angry he didn't tell her and the military about the discovery. Now she wants to test it on kids, and the military fully supports her. She's not going to stop. She doesn't care who she hurts."

"Who are the kids she's going to experiment on?" you wonder out loud.

"I don't know," she confesses, "but my husband is afraid the military will use them to create child super soldiers." You gulp and wonder if that's even legal as the car finally turns down a hidden dirt road heavily covered by trees. "I think this is it."

She drives down a winding path that's nearly invisible and would be impossible to find if you didn't know about it. There's a guard shack up ahead on the left. Behind it is a tall

metal fence surrounding a white warehouse that must be a
research facility. She stops the car.

THAT GUARD'S
NOT GOING TO LET
US THROUGH. THERE'S
NO WAY TO KNOW
IF THEY'VE TAKEN
MICHAEL IN THERE.

You figure 'Michael' must be Dr. Francis's first name.

"We have to try," you plead with her. She agrees and rolls
her window down.

"Turn around, please," the guard says. "These grounds are
for military personnel only." He's got a clipboard in his hands

and is wearing a security uniform but he's not much taller than you.

"My husband works here," Mrs. Francis tells him. "His name is Dr. Michael Francis. Go ahead and call him."

"Ma'am," he says, "I cannot discuss military matters with you. Please turn around and head back to the highway."

You realize Mrs. Francis was right and the guard's not going to let you through. There's no way to get inside … but maybe there is. You can teleport to the other side of the fence and maybe inside the warehouse. If you can verify Dr. Francis is there and is in danger, you can help him or at least let the police know.

To teleport behind the fence, turn to page 205.

To stay in the car, turn to page 215.

"YOU'LL NEVER GET AWAY WITH THIS," you tell Ava and the captain. "Let my friends go."

"Friends?" Ava asks, seeming confused. She looks through the car window and back at you. "Oh, I get it." She turns to the captain and says, "I think we found the person who destroyed our vials."

The captain laughs and replies, "Really? This kid?" as Ava pulls out a set of car keys and presses a button. The car beeps and the passenger door behind you opens. The captain shoves you into the car then slams the door shut.

You glance over the entire back seat and see there is no one here but you. The good news is Kim and Kevin are safe at home in the panic room. The bad news is you're stuck back here and the doors are locked.

Ava gets into the driver's seat and looks back at you through the rearview mirror. There is a thick wall of glass between the front and back seats, keeping you from touching anything up front. "I'm sorry," is all she says as the car pulls out of the gas station and back onto the highway.

"Why are you doing this?" you ask.

"I don't know what you've been told," she says, "but the research I'm doing will make this a better world." You doubt that's true because no one blows up a house or ties people up if they want to make the world better.

"Dr. Francis can't see clearly," she continues. "The side effects he's worried about are gifts. We can all be heroes that help each other."

"Heroes don't blow up houses," you mumble.

"Sacrifices have to be made," she argues. "I'm sorry for what's going to happen to you."

You sit back and keep quiet. You can't imagine what she plans to do. You don't want to imagine.

You've been in the car for twenty minutes when she pulls off the highway and onto a hidden dirt road. The van is still behind you as the sun begins to set.

Ava stops at an isolated security shack. A man with the same camouflaged outfit as the captain steps out with a clipboard. Ava rolls her window down and says, "I've got another one for research."

The guard looks back at you and nods at Ava then waves her and the captain through. He grabs a phone in the booth and says into it, "Get another room ready."

The car stops in front of a large white warehouse. "Don't be scared," Ava advises. "Just do what you're told and you'll be fine."

You get out of the car when the back door opens and walk with her and the captain to the front warehouse entrance. As you step inside, you see rooms with large glass windows on both sides of you. In each room is a teenager you've never seen before.

"This is the youngest one yet," the captain says, looking down at you and nudging you forward on a marble hall that never seems to end. You count seventeen teenagers as you pass them.

You reach the end of the hall and see there's one room on the right and one on the left. The one on the right makes you lose your breath. There are shelves inside with hundreds of vials full of glowing liquid like the ones you had found in Dr. Francis's secret lab.

The captain points for you to get into the room on the other side with a metal medical bed. Ava walks in with you and tells you to remain calm because she's not going to hurt you.

"We need one more," the captain says. He's right outside the room and closes the door with you and Ava inside.

Ava bangs on the glass and shouts, "What are you doing? This is my project."

The captain walks away and shouts back, "The military no longer requires your services. You are now test subject number 19."

You're not sure what to do as Ava paces the room. "This isn't supposed to happen," she mumbles. "We're supposed to change the world. Why did I trust him?" She stops and looks at you. "You can stop this."

You can't fly anymore and you're locked in this room so you're not sure how you can do anything.

"I've worked with Dr. Francis for a long time," Ava says, "and I saw some of the research on his computer. I believe I can finally make the vials work." She stands right in front of you. "I made a mistake but I can make you powerful enough to get us out of here." She motions to the rooms down the hall. "All of us."

"How?" you ask her.

She pulls a security card out of her pocket and holds it up. The captain's picture is on it. "I never completely trusted him so I swiped his card before I came into this room. It will get us out of here and into the lab across the hall."

You sense she will have you drink one of the vials, giving you another superpower. You're not sure if it would even work since you've already had one. Aside from that, the captain will notice his card is missing soon and come looking for it.

To agree to escape, turn to page 189.

To stay in the room, turn to page 209.

YOU CLOSE YOUR EYES AND FOCUS on Dr. Francis's home. You hate to leave Miguel and the other teenagers behind but they should be fine once the 911 message goes out.

You reopen your eyes and smile when you see Dr. Francis's office around you. There's still a blue towel on the table, but the bomb is gone. The secret lab is in plain view because the wall is still split open down the middle. Dr. Francis is not in here.

You step out of the office and shout his name. Your friends Kim and Kevin run up to you from the living room. Kim hugs you. Kevin gives you a fist bump. Dr. Francis appears behind them with Mrs. Francis.

"They were hiding safely in our panic room," Dr. Francis explains.

"I hate that name," Mrs. Francis says, smiling. "Safe room—please call it a safe room."

Dr. Francis winks at you and says, "Let me talk to you for a minute."

"Kids, go back to your video game and leave them alone for now," Mrs. Francis tells Kim and Kevin. "I've got to figure out what we're going to do for your birthday dinner now."

"We'll save you a spot," Kevin says to you. He faces Kim and says, "No cheating this time. Cheater."

Dr. Francis walks into the office with you and closes the door behind him as he heads for his computer desk.

"Do you want me to lock it?" you ask him, remembering

how upset he was when it wasn't locked the first time you came in here.

"No more locked doors," he says. "Have a seat." He points to the only chair at the table and faces you from his computer desk chair. "The police were here. A bomb squad took care of our little problem."

"Are you okay?" you ask him.

"I've got a few scratches, but I'll be fine," he assures you. He must see the concern on your face and explains as much as he can. "When I sent you into my lab, I also sent a signal to my family to hide in the panic ... err ... safe ... room. It's a signal with lights we've worked out over the years." He chuckles. "I also sent a distress signal to the police department. You should have seen how fast that big guy in the military uniform ran when he heard the sirens.

"I'm sure you have quite a story to tell too. It may be better if you tell it to the police first." He stands up as if he's ready to leave the room. "Oh yeah, I've notified your family about what happened earlier. They'll be here tonight. You should call them. They're worried to death."

You stand with him and head to the door. You're happy knowing his whole family is safe, but you're worried about the teenagers you left behind. You pull Miguel's cell phone out of your pocket and see the 911 text was received and police were dispatched.

"One more thing," Dr. Francis says as he opens the door. "Tell the police the truth. But please consider that if the world knows about these powers, then they could fall into the wrong hands. All I want to do is cure sickness and disease."

You listen to Kim and Kevin argue about the game they're playing. Mrs. Francis asks who wants pizza for their birthday dinner because the food she made is ruined. And there's only one thing you can say to Dr. Francis.

"Your secret's safe with me."

THE END

YOU GO INTO THE ROOM with Dr. Francis to help any way you can. The door is locked behind you with no way out.

"Are you here?" Dr. Francis asks.

"Yes, sir," you answer.

"I wish you had stayed out there," he says. "I'm sorry you're involved with all of this." He pauses for a moment and gasps.

"What?" you ask, looking around the room.

"Your hands," he says. "Look at your hands."

You put your hands in front of your face and can see them for the first time since you left the secret lab. The room door opens. "Oh, no." You knew the power was only temporary but this is the worst possible time for it to go away.

Ava steps into the room and calls the captain back. "Who is this kid?" she asks him.

He shrugs and says, "I put the captain in here by himself. There was no one else here."

Ava seems confused, but her eyes light up. "It works," she whispers. "Captain, put the kid in another room. I have many experiments to run." He grabs your arm before you can get away.

"Don't fight it," Ava warns you. "This is where you were always meant to be." She stares at your arms and legs as the captain leads you away. "You're just the right age and size. You couldn't be any more perfect."

"For what?" you ask.

An old man in a lab coat steps into the room and jabs you

in the arm with a syringe. "You won't remember anything in just a minute," Ava predicts. The room around you is getting blurry. You feel exhausted. "You will be the most feared soldier ever known."

>>time travel back to page 139<<
THE END

YOU SIT BACK AND WAIT for what feels like forever for Shannon to come back. "Good to see you again, Phil," she says to him as she gets into the car. "We should get together sometime."

"Whatever," he says, shaking his head and motioning for the car the turn around.

"I hate that guy," she admits to you. "Why didn't you use your magic and teleport into the shack?" Her eyes get big as two soldiers appear and stand in front of the gate.

"It doesn't work anymore," you say with your arms crossed.

"That's too bad," she replies as the car gets back onto the highway. She drives you to the Francises' house and makes sure everyone is safe before leaving.

"I'm glad you're here," Kevin says. "I was afraid we wouldn't see you again."

"Where's our dad?" Kim asks.

"I'm sorry," you tell her honestly. "I couldn't save him. I can't teleport anymore."

"You have nothing to apologize for," Mrs. Francis says. You can't help but feel that's not true. You should have tried to get into the guard shack.

>>time travel back to page 143<<
THE END

YOU WALK INTO THE LAB across from you and grab the vial Ava has been mixing with the green and red liquids. It must be something important because she was taken away after reading Dr. Francis's notes about it and then creating it. The liquid is green with a glow now.

The front warehouse door opens again and you hear one set of heavy footsteps heading toward you. You know it's the captain. You swallow the liquid in the vial as quickly as you can.

The captain is staring at you through the glass now. You put your hands up and hope he doesn't hurt you when he takes you away. He walks into the lab and stops in front of you.

You gulp.

He looks around the room and shakes his head before he goes to the computer and shuts it down. Can he see you? You wave your hands and stick your tongue out at him but he doesn't notice.

You are invisible!

You notice a keycard attached to his belt and realize that's how the room doors open. The beeping sound you heard earlier was from someone swiping a keycard in front of the room door.

You quietly unclip the card from his belt before he can leave. You step outside the room and swipe the card in front of a digital display. The room door closes before the captain can get out.

"No!" he shouts as he bangs a fist against the glass. You

hurry down the hall and swipe the card in front of every door to let the teenagers out.

"Hey," you say to Miguel. He looks around because he can't tell where the voice is coming from. "It's me. The kid you talked to on the bus. I'm invisible."

"This day just gets weirder and weirder," he says. "What's up?" You ask him if he has a cell phone. He pulls one out of his pocket and holds it in front of him. "Yeah, but there's no signal in here. They've jammed it or something."

You grab the cellphone from him because you've got an idea. His eyes are bugged out because the cellphone looks like it's floating. You remember reading that 911 can be texted from some areas for emergencies when it's not possible to call. You send a text with the approximate area and the number of teens held captive here. You have no idea if it will go out but hope for the best.

You hand the cell phone back to Miguel and ask him to gather all the other teens together. You tell them that you all need to work together to get out of here because you're stronger together than working alone. They're weirded out that your voice has no body.

Before you can say anything else, the front warehouse door opens. Two soldiers walk in and stare at the teens.

"Get back you in your rooms!" one of them shouts. "All of you! Now!"

The teens stand firm, refusing to back down. You hear sirens in the distance and they're getting closer.

The soldiers turn around and run out the front door. Three police cars pull up in front of the warehouse at that exact moment. Officers jump out of the cars and arrest the soldiers.

The teens are taken away by ambulances to make sure they're safe. "Thanks," Miguel says to you. "That's twice today you saved me. I owe you one." It's when he shakes your hand you realize you're not invisible anymore.

Dr. Francis meets you in the parking lot with a police officer. "You texted 911, huh? That's pretty cool." He holds up a hand and gives you five.

The back doors of the police car open and Kim, Kevin, and Mrs. Francis step out. They rush up to you. Kim hugs you and Kevin salutes you.

"We're all friends, right?" Kim asks.

"Friends for life," you and Kevin say at the same time.

You saved Dr. Francis.
You saved the bus.
You saved the teens.
You stopped the bad guys.
You made sure your friends were safe.

You are officially a superhero!

THE END

YOU STAY IN THE CAR with Dr. Francis and make sure your seatbelt is tight. He drives the Nova back onto the dirt road and revs the car as fast as he can. You roll your window up, thinking it'll protect you somehow.

The trees around you pass faster and faster. The guard shack is on your left now. Your stomach is in knots as a guard jumps out and waves his arms wildly at you to stop.

"Hold on tight!" the doctor yells as the metal gate gets closer and closer.

Here it comes…

Breathe…

Sparks fly in front of you as the Nova crashes through the gate. Your whole body is jolted from the impact. You brace against your door as the car skids in front of a white warehouse—the research facility.

Two soldiers rush out of a small wooden cabin next to the facility to keep you out of it. The guard you passed in the shack joins them.

"Find your family," you tell Dr. Francis before you jump out of the car and face the soldiers. They're not intimidated by you and laugh. You rip the passenger door off the car and throw it in front of them.

The soldiers and the guard look at each other, shake their heads, then run off to a nearby Jeep and drive away like they're being chased by angry hornets.

You look back to the Nova and see the doctor is gone. He must be inside the facility and you've got to join him. You open the entrance door and see a long marble hallway in front of you. There are rooms on both sides of the hallway with large glass windows. No one is in the rooms you see.

Dr. Francis is lying on the floor, ten feet away. You rush to him and see that he can't move.

"Keep your eyes open," he says quietly. "Dr. Brown is a dangerous man. Stay away from his needle."

"Your family," you say, bending down next to him. "Where are they?"

"The last room on the right," he says. "They may be there. It's where all this began."

"I'll come back for you," you assure him, standing to your feet.

"Wait," he says. "Pink." You're not sure what he means but it's too late to ask. He passed out or fell asleep.

You march to the end of the hallway and look through the window to the room on the right. Inside is a lab much larger than the one in Dr. Francis's. The walls are lined with dozens, maybe hundreds of vials just like his, filled with colorful liquid that's not glowing. Ava is inside, working on the stolen computer from Dr. Francis's office.

You try to open the door but it won't budge. There's a panel on the outside that uses some kind of keycard.

"Need help?" a man's voice calls out from behind you.

You turn and see a man in a white lab coat with a syringe in his hand, squirting liquid from it up into the air. He jabs it at your arm, but you bat it away. The syringe flies through the air and shatters on the marble floor.

Dr. Brown backs away from you and runs down the hall, right out the front door. You snatched the keycard from his belt before he took off.

You swipe the keycard on the outside panel and the door opens. Ava stands up from her chair and puts her hands in the air.

"I'm glad you're here," she says. "We can change the world together." She glances at the window behind you, and you notice the captain outside the room, heading for the door. He shakes his head at you.

All of the vials on the walls around you have liquid with various colors. There are at least three of each color. All except for one. There's only one vial with glowing orange liquid.

You realize what Dr. Francis meant with his last word before passing out. Orange. Drink from the orange vial. There's something he knows about the orange liquid that may save you. But you may not have enough time to get to it because the captain just swiped his keycard on the door panel.

To get the pink vial, turn to page 202.

To defend yourself, turn to page 214.

THE CAPTAIN RIPS THE GUARD'S KEYCARD from your hand then tosses you into the room across from Dr. Francis's. Ava and an old man in a lab coat enter your room. The man has a syringe in his hand and squeezes liquid from it up into the air.

"You will be our first little super soldier," Ava says to you. "You will be the most feared child in the world." The old man steps forward and jabs you in the arm with his needle.

You yawn and sit on the metal bed as Ava stares at you. "You won't have any memories of this day," she continues. "You won't remember who you are or where you're from. Thank you for volunteering."

The room grows dark and cold. What did she mean when she said ....

>>time travel back to page 149<<
THE END

YOU TELEPORT BACK TO YOUR HOUSE and tell the twins what happened. "She's going to be okay," you assure them. You wanted to go with Mrs. Francis but she was going exactly where Dr. Francis had said not to go. After thinking about it, you couldn't go with her.

It's getting dark now and she hasn't called or come back here. Hours have passed. Kim and Kevin are wide awake with you. He's staring out the window and she's waiting by the phone.

You hope Dr. and Mrs. Francis are safe but you will never see them again. Whatever happens from this point on, you're never going to leave your friends.

>>time travel back to page 134<<
THE END

AVA WAVES THE SECURITY CARD over a sensor by the door. It opens and the two of you peek down the hall to make sure the captain doesn't see you before you dash across the hall to the lab. She waves her card again and that door opens.

You rush inside and admire the hundreds of vials on the walls. They are full of liquid with all the colors of the rainbow.

"Give me two minutes," Ava says as she powers up the computer. At that very moment you see the captain across the hall, looking into the empty room you came from. He turns to face you and his eyes get big.

"What are you doing?" he shouts as he bangs his fists against the lab glass. "Get out of there!"

"Hurry," you tell Ava as the captain races back down the hall for help.

"Almost there," she says, reading the computer notes as fast as she can. "Got it!" She races to a shelf and pulls off two vials. One has green liquid in it and one has red liquid. "All I have to do is put a few drops of red into the green. I should've known. It was right in front of me the entire time."

Heavy footsteps race down the hall toward you. It sounds like at least three soldiers.

"You don't have to do this," Ava says, mixing the vial. "I don't know for sure what effect it will have on you."

Three soldiers are in front of the door now. One is swiping his card.

You snatch the mixed vial from Ava and swallow its

contents in one big gulp as the soldiers rush in. You freeze when they stand in front of you.

"Where'd the kid go?" the captain asks, searching the room. Ava shrugs.

You realize you are invisible and no one can see you. The vial worked!

"Get her out of here," the captain orders the other soldiers about Ava. "Make her Test Subject number 1."

It occurs to you that the only way in and out of these rooms is with the security keycards. You work as fast as you can to take the cards from every soldier as they march Ava out of the room.

Since Ava is out first and you're right behind her now, you swipe a card from outside the door to shut all the soldiers in behind you.

"We're safe now," you tell Ava. She looks around her, wondering where your voice came from.

"You're invisible," Ava says in astonishment. "I always believed it could work but I had my doubts." She sighs. "I'm sorry for what I did to you."

You hand her a keycard. "Let the other kids out," you say. "All of them."

You call Dr. Francis and the police from Ava's cell phone. Dr. Francis confirms that the twins and his wife are safe and out of the panic room. The police arrest the captain, the soldiers, and Ava.

"Thank you," Ava says. She can see you now because you're

no longer invisible. "You saved me."

You saved Ava.
You saved Dr. Francis.
You saved strangers.
You made sure your friends were safe.

You are officially a superhero!

THE END

YOU CLOSE YOUR EYES AND FOCUS on the outside of the research facility as best as you can remember it. You reopen them and you're staring at a large bus. This is the bus Miguel and his friends came here in. The facility is right behind you.

You check Miguel's cell phone and see it has two bars now. The 911 text is sending ... sending ... sent!

Over to your right is the wooden cabin Miguel said the soldiers came from. You tiptoe over and see through a side window that they're watching a football game.

You hurry back to facility's entrance and open the door. The teenagers are standing just inside, waiting for you. You motion for them to get back on the bus quietly. You have no idea how long it will take police to respond but you can't wait around to find out.

"Hey," Miguel says. "That's everyone. Except for a weird dude in a lab coat that tried to inject one of my friends with something. We shoved him into a room and locked it." The captain must have let him out on his way to the lab earlier.

You're the last person on the bus and ask where the driver is. "Dude," Miguel says. "One of those military guys drove us here. We thought he was just a weirdo in a costume."

"I drive my mom's van," a girl says from a seat in the back. "Let me try it." She comes up front and jumps when the bus roars to life. "Yeah, this is nothing like the van."

The two soldiers run out of their cabin and shout for you to stop. You close the bus doors before they get here. They bang their fists on the bus and keep shouting for you to get out. Maybe you should because no one on the bus can drive this thing.

To get off the bus, turn to page 210.

To stay on the bus, turn to page 218.

YOU WALK FURTHER DOWN THE HALL as the captain leaves the building. There is one teenager in every room you pass. Now you're at the end of the hall and on the right side is a huge lab that looks exactly like Dr. Francis's secret lab. Ava is inside.

She looks through the window for a moment like she can see you and makes a phone call. She comes to the door, opens it, looks directly at you and says, "Can I help you?"

You realize you're not invisible anymore when the captain picks you up from behind and carries you into the lab. The door closes and locks behind him.

"Where did this kid come from?" Ava asks the captain. He shrugs. "No matter." She looks over your arms and legs. "Perfect age. Perfect weight. Perfect for my experiments."

The walls are lined with colorful vials like the ones in Dr. Francis's lab but they don't glow. Ava is trying to recreate what he created and that's why they brought him here. She has one vial in her hand that has black glowing liquid in it. "I think I've figured it out. We'll test it on the kid soon enough." She sets the vial in a holder on her desk.

The captain sets you down and you immediately stomp on his foot. You run to Ava's desk and take the vial out of the holder.

"Don't…" she starts to say.

You flick the cap off and swallow the black liquid in one big gulp. You don't feel any different like when you drank from the green vial in Dr. Francis's lab.

The captain marches toward you. You avoid him until you're backed up against the door. He reaches out to grab you but somehow your body passes through the door like it's not even there. You're on the other side now, looking at the captain through the door. You reach your hands through the door like a ghost and quickly grab the security keycards from the captain and Ava. They can't get out now.

You go back to Dr. Francis's room to let him out. He's shocked to see you when the door opens. You explain what happened and prepare to leave with him.

"We need to get the others out," he says. You agree and give him one of the security keycards. The two of you open every room and let the teenagers out.

Two soldiers enter the facility. The teenagers hold them back and lock them in a room. Now the teenagers are getting on the party bus outside.

"It was supposed to be a fun day," one teenager says to you. "I'm Miguel. Thank you for saving us."

You and the doctor get on the bus with the teens so they can drop you off at Dr. Francis's house. Kim and Kevin are waiting outside when you get there.

You're glad your friends are safe. But there's one thing you can't get over. "I'm sorry about your mom."

"What's there to be sorry about?" a voice says from behind you. You turn to see Mrs. Francis and hug her.

"I don't understand," you tell her. "How are you here? The bomb...."

"Don't you know my husband's a genius?" she asks, winking at him.

"Yeah, but how…" you say.

"We have a lifetime to tell our stories, thanks to you," she says. "We owe you everything. You are our hero."

THE END

YOU GET OUT OF THE CAR quietly and leave your door open as you head for the guard shack. Shannon keeps an arm around Phil so he can't turn and see you.

You step inside the guard shack and slide the door closed. Inside is a white desk with a black swivel chair in front of it. To the side is a tall cabinet that opens with doors. Next to that is a miniature refrigerator and microwave. The thing that catches your eye the most is the remote keypad sitting on top of the microwave.

You grab the keypad and press the button that says, "Open Gate." The metal gate outside begins to open.

"What are you doing?" Phil shouts, running back to the shack. "Close it!" You keep the keypad and race back to the car with Phil shouting at you so stop the whole time.

Shannon jumps into the driver's seat, slams her door shut, and presses a button on the dashboard that locks all the doors. "We don't have much time," she says, out of breath. "That guy hates me." She zooms through the open gate while Phil waves his arms at you in frustration.

The yellow sports car and camouflaged military van are close now, parked in front of the warehouse. Shannon skids the security car in front of the warehouse at a dangerous speed. Your heart is racing as you get out with her and approach the building.

You both freeze when you open the warehouse door and cold air hits your faces. In front of you is a long marble hallway with rooms that have large windows on both sides of it. Each room has a metal medical bed in it—nothing else.

"We've got to find him," you urge, rushing down the hall and looking into each room's window. Shannon senses what you're doing and looks on one side of the hall while you look on the other. You find Dr. Francis looking back at you through one room's window. "He's in here!" you shout to Shannon.

You try to open the door but it's locked with a security keycard panel by the knob.

"Stand back," Shannon orders. You step aside as she attempts to kick the door down. She grabs her leg in pain after the door doesn't budge. "No more tacos," she promises herself.

"There' got to be a way in," you say. "Keep looking." You're working as fast as possible because Ava and the captain are here somewhere. Maybe another room will give you a clue about how to get in and get the doctor out.

You're at the last room on the right side now. Ava is inside, mixing vials of colorful liquid in what looks like a large lab. She doesn't see you.

The door behind you opens and someone steps out. You turn in surprise as an old man in a lab coat charges at you with a syringe. You instinctively raise your hands in front of you in defense.

"Not today!" Shannon shouts from behind him. She karate chops the side of his neck and watches him crash to the floor. "That's right. Don't mess with the best." She looks at you and nods. "I hate needles." She snatches the keycard off the lab guy's belt and hands it to you. "I believe this is what you're looking for."

Now you can get Dr. Francis out of his room and hopefully make it out of here without any more trouble. Your gut tells you that you may need to go into the lab first and stop Ava from what she's doing.

To get Dr. Francis out of his room,
turn to page 211.

To stop Ava,
turn to page 219.

YOU DART OUT OF THE ROOM and run down the hall as fast as you can to get out of this warehouse. You feel bad for leaving the teenagers behind as they bang on their windows when you pass them, begging for your help. You've got to focus on saving yourself for now.

You're almost to the front door. Your heart is racing but you're relieved. You'll be out of here soon and send help back for the others.

Someone pulls the door open from outside and sunlight hits your face, blinding you. You freeze and shield your eyes with your hand.

"What are you doing here?" a deep voice calls out. You know it belongs to the captain.

You can't breathe. You've been caught. You turn and try to run back, but a large hand reaches out and grabs your shirt.

"You're not going anywhere," the captain says. He keeps ahold of your shirt and forces you to walk with him in the same direction you came from. "Who are you? How did you even get in here?"

You don't answer him as you pass the rooms with teenagers again. Some have their heads down. Some are shaking their heads, looking ashamed of you. Others are banging their fists on the glass in anger.

The captain stops you at the room on the end, the same one you hid in. He tosses you in and says, "We needed another test subject. You're just the right age and size." He pulls a security keycard from his belt and swipes it over a panel on the outside door.

The door beeps then closes and locks you in. You stare at the lab across from your room as the captain walks away and wish you had drunk from another vial.

You're trapped here for the rest of your life.

>>time travel back to page 163<<
THE END

YOU GRAB THE PINK VIAL, flick the cap off, and swallow the contents as the captain rushes in and tries to stop you. He snatches your arm and pulls you away from the shelves. You push your hands against his chest like you did before but nothing happens this time.

Your strength is gone.

Did you make a huge mistake by drinking the from the pink vial? Did Dr. Francis mean something else when he said Pink? The captain takes you out of the room and you pass Dr. Francis. He's awake again.

"They're not here," he says with a smile when he sees you without Mrs. Francis, Kim, and Kevin. "My family isn't here. They're safe." He appears to be fading in and out.

You're tossed into one of the rooms and locked in. You watch from your window as teenagers are marched down the hall and thrown into individual rooms. Dr. Francis is put into the room directly across from yours.

You sit on the cold metal medical bed in your room and wonder if you made the right decisions. Your door opens and Ava, the captain, and Dr. Brown walk in. The doctor has a new syringe in his hand.

"I'm sorry it has to be this way," Ava lies. "We don't know what you drank and we have to protect ourselves from you. You will never be able to move again." She nods to the captain. He grabs your shoulders and holds you in place.

The doctor squirts liquid from his syringe and moves toward you. Whatever he's about to inject you with is going to paralyze you for the rest of your life.

"Stop!" you yell.

The three of them freeze in place. You think they're mocking you but they don't even blink. You walk around them, studying their faces and arms completely frozen. "How is this possible?" you whisper. You figure they'll be like this until your new power wears off. You swipe a keycard on the inside door panel and walk out.

The teenagers are moving in their rooms and you understand you only stopped time in the room you were in. You've got to let the teenagers out or they'll be experimented on like you were about to be. There's only one choice to make here.

You run down one side of the hall with your keycard out, swiping every panel you pass. The doors open one after another, and teenagers step out. Now you're running down the other side. The teenagers are cheering for you with every step you take.

They're all out now.

"Can someone help carry my friend, Dr. Francis, please?" you ask them.

Two boys carry him outside with everyone else. You all get onto a bus that's waiting out front. This must be how they got here.

"We were on our way to a water park," one boy in a swimsuit and tank top says. "My name's Miguel." He uses a cell phone to call the police.

Several police cars with sirens blaring and lights flashing pass the bus after it's on the main road. You and the teenagers cheer for them.

You and Dr. Francis are dropped off at a hospital so he can be checked out. You call his family, surprised you're able to reach them, and let them know where you are.

Kim hugs you and Kevin fist bumps you when they get here. Mrs. Francis also hugs you and thanks you for whatever you did to make sure her husband was safe.

"This is one birthday we'll never forget," she says to all of you.

"And we still have a video game to finish playing," Kevin reminds you and Kim. He looks directly at her. "No cheating this time, cheater."

THE END

YOU CLOSE YOUR EYES AND PICTURE the space between the metal fence and the white warehouse. Now open your eyes.

There's a large party bus next to you. Did you come to the right place? You turn around and verify the metal fence is behind you. The white warehouse is also in front of you. "What's that bus doing here?" you whisper.

You walk to the warehouse and stand at the front door. "Here's the moment of truth," you say under your breath as you pull the door open.

Cold air hits your face as you stare down a long marble hallway. You step inside and notice there are rooms all along both sides of the hallway. The rooms have large windows for viewing whatever's inside.

A teenager bangs his fists on the room window closest to you. He looks like he's shouting for help but you can't hear anything—not his voice and not the pounding on the glass. The room he's in has a medical bed and equipment that looks like it came from a hospital.

You walk slowly down the hall and notice every room has a teenager in it. They all appear desperate to escape. You'll help them if you can, but right now you're looking for Dr. Francis.

You reach the end of the hall and look to the room on your right. You can't believe your eyes. The room is set up as a large lab that looks just like the one that was in Dr. Francis's house. The walls are lined with vials of colorful liquid that don't glow like the ones you destroyed. Ava is sitting at a computer. Dr.

Francis is tied to a chair.

You try to open the door to get inside but it's locked. There's a panel on the outside that must require some type of keycard. You close your eyes and teleport inside.

"How did you get in here?" Ava says, standing up from her chair. You look to Dr. Francis and try to figure out how you can get him untied. "Oh, I see. Whoever you are, you've had the medication and it works. Forget about him," she says, nodding to the doctor. "You and I can change the world together."

"Don't listen to her," Dr. Francis warns, sounding exhausted.

"I can give you everything you ever wanted," Ava claims.

The room door opens and the captain enters. You close your eyes and try to teleport out of the room, but it doesn't work. The captain marches toward you with a large grin on his face.

"Purple!" Doctor Francis shouts. "Drink the purple one!" You only see one purple vial in the room and race to the wall it's on. The liquid is glowing in a way you recognize.

"Stop the kid!" Ava shouts.

The captain lumbers after you as you reach the vial, flick the cap off, and swallow the liquid in one huge gulp. He grabs your shoulders and pulls you away from the wall.

You're not sure what the purple liquid does, but you try to get away from the captain by pushing him back. His body flies through the air and crashes into the wall with the large window.

You stare at your hands, wondering how you did that.

Ava runs to the captain to make sure he's okay. You watch them as you untie the doctor and lead him to the door.

"Don't go," Ava pleads. "Don't you see all the good you can do? We can make the military stronger. You can be a part of that." You ignore her and bend down to snatch the captain's keycard from him.

As soon as you step out of the room, a man in a lab coat rushes at you. He's got a syringe in his hand and tries to stab your arm with it. The needle bends and breaks when it presses against your skin. The man is startled and runs away screaming.

You head for the exit with your arm around the doctor for support. "We can't leave them behind," he says, nodding to the teens in all the rooms around you. You know he's right and use the captain's keycard to unlock every room as you pass it.

Two soldiers enter the warehouse and yell at everyone to get back in their rooms. You grab the soldiers by their shirt collars, lift them into the air, and hit their heads together. They slump to the floor in a daze.

The teens cheer for you and thank you as they run out the front door and get back on the bus they were sent here on.

You walk with Dr. Francis to the metal gate and use all your strength to push it open with your hands. Mrs. Francis is on the other side and jumps out of her car. She rushes to her husband and embraces him.

You look at the guard in the shack and pound your fists together. He slides the door closed and crouches down to hide behind it.

The bus beeps at you and the teens cheer for you as they drive away from the research facility, or warehouse, or whatever you want to call it.

Mrs. Francis hugs you. "You saved him. You saved all of them." She leads you and Dr. Francis to the car. "Hey," she says before you get into the back seat. "You're a superhero."

THE END

YOU STAY IN THE ROOM because the captain will be angry if he catches you trying to escape. It's safer in here for now.

Ava slips across the hall and is working on a computer in the lab. You want to trust her, but even Dr. Francis warned you about her.

A teenager down the hall screams. You strain to see down the hall from the glass window and see an old man in a lab coat walk out of the room closest to the front door. He has a syringe in his hand and is squirting liquid out of it as he moves to the next room.

More screams. What's he doing to those teenagers? What's in the syringe? The screams become louder as they get closer and closer to your room.

Soldiers burst into the lab across from you and arrest Ava. She mouths, "Sorry," to you as they march her down the hall.

Your door opens and the man in the lab coat steps in. He squirts a stream of liquid straight up into the air from the syringe.

Maybe you could have helped Ava. Maybe you could have saved her. Maybe you could have saved the other prisoners. You don't know what's happened to your friends. You're never getting out of here. If only you could go back…

>>time travel back to page 174<<
THE END

THE TEENAGERS VOTE TO GET OFF the bus because at least they'll have food and water inside. You don't think this is a good idea but you go along with it so you're not alone. You make sure you're the last person off.

You close your eyes and teleport to the front of the cabin the two soldiers came from. "Hey! Over here!" you shout to them.

They face you and appear confused. One soldier pats the other on the chest as a signal to come get you. That soldier marches toward you quickly.

The teenagers cheer for you and knock down the soldier with them. They tie his hands up with a white tank top.

When the other soldier approaches you, you teleport directly behind him. "Over here," you taunt.

He turns and tries to grab you, but you teleport again behind him. "Too slow." You're getting better at this because you don't have to close your eyes anymore.

He grimaces in frustration right as sirens fill the air. "This is too weird," he says, exasperated. "I'm outta here."

"No you're not," Miguel says, blocking him with five other teenagers.

Police arrive and arrest the soldiers. They inform you that Dr. Francis is safe and a bomb squad diffused the bomb. His wife and kids were hiding in a safe room and are fine. Miguel and the teens thank you for saving them.

THE END

YOU SWIPE THE KEYCARD on Dr. Francis's door and let him out. His body is frail from whatever they did to him. Shannon helps support his weight while you rush down the marble hallway to escape from this nightmare.

The front warehouse door opens before you reach it and two soldiers enter with the captain. Phil joins them and points at you. "That's them," he says to the soldiers.

Ava steps out of the lab at the other end of the hallway and walks in your direction.

"I'm not going out," Shannon says. "Not like this." She seats the doctor against the wall and puts her fists up toward the soldiers. "Okay, who's first?"

Phil cracks his neck and steps forward. Shannon punches a fist at his chest, but he bats it away and laughs.

"You think that's funny?" Shannon says. "At least my fly's not open."

Phil looks down at his pant zipper at the same moment Shannon gives him an uppercut to his chin. He lands on his rear end and looks around like he has no idea where he's at.

"That's right," Shannon says, moving her shoulders up and down in victory and daring the soldiers to come at her. "I had forty hours of training."

"Shannon!" you shout as Ava appears and jabs a needle into her arm. She slumps to the floor, unconscious.

"Put the doctor in the lab with me," Ava orders the soldiers. "No time for games." She looks at you and her eyes light up. "Put this kid and the security guard in their own rooms." She heads back down the hall to the lab.

"Wait!" you shout at her. "Why are you doing this?"

She stops and walks back to you as the captain grabs your arm. "Imagine a world where you don't have to think for yourself," she says. "I'm creating child super soldiers with no memory of who they were before." She looks at you from head to toe. "You're just the right height and weight. You'll be the first."

The captain tosses you into a room and watches as the man in the lab coat enters. He's got the same needle he attacked you with earlier and jabs you in the arm with it. They both leave and lock you in.

How did you get here? What's your name? You don't remember anything before this moment.

>>time travel back to page 199<<
THE END

YOU FLY AWAY FROM THE BOMB and the bus as fast as you can. There's no way you can stop the bomb. You hope the bus doesn't get hit by it and no one is hurt, but there's nothing you can do if anything bad happens.

You hear the bomb explode behind you and keep flying. You sincerely hope no one is hurt.

You're exhausted from flying and carrying that bomb. Your arms feel like they're on fire. You head down to the ground so you can rest.

Your feet land clumsily and you stumble into a wet pile of cement. You're on your knees and you put your hands down for balance. They sink into the same cement.

You try to pull your hands out, but it's nearly impossible because you're so tired now. You can't move your legs because your knees are resting in the setting cement.

A large cement truck's engine revs up from behind you and the truck drives away.

"Hey!" you shout. "Help!"

The truck keeps going and is out of sight now. You notice an unopened bag of cement next to you. The words on it say, "Lou's Super Duper Quick Dry Cement."

You could be stuck out here all night. You take a deep breath and wonder if this is karma. You didn't help the people on the bus and now there's no one to help you.

>>time travel back to page 65<<
THE END

YOU HOLD THE DOOR CLOSED so the captain can't get inside. Your feet are slipping as he pushes against it. Somehow, he's stronger than you now.

Ava stands over you as you crouch with your back against the door. "I've got bad news for you. Your strength is disappearing. How sad." She watches as the door slides open more and more and you lose your footing.

The captain is in the room. He grabs your shoulders and lifts you up into the air. "Not so strong after all," he taunts. He forces you out of the lab and back down the hall. You pass Dr. Francis, still on the floor, fading in and out.

"They're not here," he says with a smile. "My family isn't here. They're safe."

The captain leads you to a room, shoves you inside, and locks the door. You watch through your window as he throws Dr. Francis into the room across from yours.

A group of teenagers are marched down the hall at the same time. They are thrown into individual rooms.

You sit on the cold metal medical bed in your room and wonder if you made the right decisions. You don't have powers anymore. You're nothing more than a lab rat now. And you'll be trapped here for the rest of your life.

>>time travel back to page 186<<
THE END

YOU STAY IN YOUR SEAT as Mrs. Francis turns the car around and heads home. "We'll tell the police about this place," she says. "That can't be the end of this … it can't."

Kim and Kevin are excited to see you and their mom when you get back to the house. "Where's Daddy?" Kim asks. Mrs. Francis explains that she doesn't know but they'll find him— she's sure of it.

You hope they find Dr. Francis one day, but you'll never know. Mrs. Francis gets a hotel room for her and the kids but they disappear soon after and you never hear from them again.

>>time travel back to page 170<<
THE END

YOU WAIT WITH DR. FRANCIS as the police and paramedics arrive. A firetruck, ambulance, and police car are in front of the house and their sirens are deafening.

"Step over here," one officer says, pulling the two of you away from the yard as the fire department goes to work. "Tell me what happened." He's holding a notepad.

"Someone broke into my house and blew it up," Dr. Francis says in frustration.

"Was anyone else in the house?" the officer asks.

Dr. Francis seems hesitant but explains his family is in a panic room. You raise your hand to show you were there too.

"Do you live here?" the officer asks you.

You shake your head and point across the street. Another police officer joins the first one and whispers something.

The officer that's been questioning you folds his notebook closed and says, "Dr. Francis, I'm going to need you and this kid to come downtown with us to answer some questions."

"Aren't we already doing that?" Dr. Francis asks. "I need to be here when my family comes out."

"There's some concern that your house blew up while you and this kid are the only ones who seem to be unharmed," the officer says. "It looks like your family is hiding from you for protection."

"That's not how it is," Dr. Francis argues. "You think I did this? My assistant did this."

"Okay," the officer says. "Let's go talk about it." The two officers guide Dr. Francis and you to their squad car and put

put you in the back seat.

This is going to take way too much time. You may never see your friends again. You had an extraordinary power and you didn't use it.

>>time travel back to page 31<<
THE END

YOU AND THE TEENAGERS REFUSE to leave the bus after a long vote with a lot of disagreement. The girl who drives her mom's van has figured out how to make the bus go forward. Backwards and other directions might be a problem.

"Everyone, hold on tight," she says as she turns the bus around and heads away from the facility faster and faster. The other teenagers cheer for her as the soldiers fade behind you.

A line of police cars with sirens blaring and lights flashing passes the bus as they head for the facility. Everyone on the bus cheers louder for the police.

Miguel is in the seat behind you and puts a hand on your shoulder. "You saved us."

The teenagers drop you off at Dr. Francis's house. Your friends Kim and Kevin meet you at the door and hug you. You wonder where they've been. Dr. and Mrs. Francis welcome you back.

"We have a lot to tell you," Kim says. "So much has happened." The family explains how they hid in a secure safe room when Ava and the captain came. How the police showed up and diffused the bomb. How everyone was looking for you.

"That's amazing," you tell them. "I'm glad you're all okay."

"Enough about us," Dr. Francis says. "Tell us what happened to you."

THE END

YOU SWIPE THE KEYCARD on the lab door panel and enter to face Ava. "Can I help you?" she asks, leery.

"I came for Dr. Francis," you inform her. "And to stop you." Her eyes move from side to side like she's trying to solve a puzzle.

"This place is freaky," Shannon says when she joins you, looking at the colorful vials all around you.

"I wasn't aware that we have new security," Ava says sarcastically.

"I wasn't aware that you're mean and petty," Shannon replies as the captain enters the room.

You glimpse the one vial in this lab that has glowing yellow liquid in it. When Ava was mixing vials earlier, she mixed equal parts red and green together. You recall the yellow residue in the vial that the mouse in Dr. Francis's office drank from.

You dart to that vial on the wall, uncap it, and swallow the contents. The captain tries to grab you, but you zip from one side of the room to the other faster than lightning. You zip from Ava to the captain, taking their keycards from them. You zip to Shannon's side and whisper, "Run."

She hoofs it out of the room while the captain and Ava try to figure out how to catch you. You zip out with Shannon and lock the door, trapping the captain and Ava inside.

You go straight to Dr. Francis's door and let him out. Two soldiers and Phil enter the warehouse. "That's them!" Phil shouts. "Get them!"

Shannon puts her fists up to fight. You zip around the

soldiers and Phil, tie their shoelaces together, and watch them fall on top of each other like dominoes as they try to get to you.

You and Shannon help Dr. Francis back to the security car and drive away. She drops you and Dr. Francis off at your house.

"Thank you," Dr. Francis says. He winks at you. "Both of you. You saved my life."

Mrs. Francis, Kim, and Kevin rush out of your house and nearly knock the doctor over. They all thank you before going into the house to tell each other their stories.

"You should come inside," you tell Shannon. "You're a hero. I couldn't have done this without you."

"Not this time," she says. "I've got to go study for my state officer certification. And maybe grab a few tacos." She chuckles and salutes you before driving away.

Your friends are urging you to come inside. They're happy to be together again and it's all because of you. You are a true superhero.

THE END

YOU REFUSE TO LET GO OF THE BOMB because you can't let anyone get hurt. You ignore the beeping as the last seconds count down.

You're over the lake now. There's only one second left. You drop the bomb and it sinks.

The bomb explodes and shoots water full force into the sky at you, blasting you backward and into the lake. You fight to stay above the water because your body is exhausted. You try to fly out but can't anymore.

A fisherman pulls you out of the water and lays you in his boat. You cough out what feels like a bucket of water. "You're gonna be okay, kid. Glad I got here in time."

You wonder what Ava meant when she said she had experiments to run on the children. You can only hope that Dr. Francis or the police can help them. There's no way you can find them now.

>>time travel back to page 43<<
THE END

A note to all kids and parents

Thank you so much for taking the time to read this story! You're Awesome! You're Super! I hope you enjoyed reading this as much as I enjoyed writing it, and I'd be eternally grateful if you'd leave a review on Amazon and Goodreads to let me know what you think about **Select Your Superpower**. Your review helps other readers like yourself find this book and enjoy it.

Be sure to click the Follow button next to my name (David Blaze) on Amazon to be notified when my sequels and new books are released.

You can find me on Facebook as:
David Blaze, Children's Author

You can find my books and contact me at:
www.davidblazebooks.com

Check out these other award-winning books for young readers by David Blaze!

MY
fox ①
ATE MY
HOMEWORK

DAVID BLAZE

MY
fox
ATE MY
CAKE

DAVID BLAZE

MY
fox
ATE MY
ALARM CLOCK

DAVID BLAZE

MY
fox
Begins

DAVID BLAZE

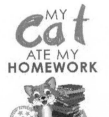

MY
cat
ATE MY
HOMEWORK

DAVID BLAZE

MY
fox
ATE MY
REPORT CARD

DAVID BLAZE

MY
fox
MY FRIEND
FOREVER

DAVID BLAZE

JANIE
GETS A GENIE
FOR CHRISTMAS

DAVID BLAZE

About the Author

Timothy David and his son Zander Blaze live in Orlando, Florida with their crazy dog (Sapphire) and Zander's awesome mom! Timothy David loves to watch funny movies and eat pizza rolls! Zander Blaze loves to play video games and feast on chicken nuggets! Together, as David Blaze, they share lots of laughs and have lots of fun.

Wow! That's Super!

David Blaze

Manufactured by Amazon.ca
Bolton, ON

28213949R00136